ENOUGH TO KILL A HORSE

Fanny Lynam's party was awkward to arrange. Clare Forwood wasn't eager to come, even though she had particularly asked to meet Sir Peter Poulter, the newspaper tycoon who had already accepted. There was the risk that Tom Mordue would quarrel with everyone; and, worse of all, Fanny was nervous of the smart young widow, Laura Greensdale, who had just become engaged to her half-brother, Kit Raven.

What did Laura want with Kit, Fanny wondered? Was it true that there was something mysterious, something peculiar, about Laura? At any rate, Fanny knew that her speciality — lobster patties — would help to make the party a success . . .

ENOUGH TO KILL
A HORSE

Elizabeth Ferrars

First published 1955
by
William Collins Sons & Co. Ltd.

This edition 2002 by Chivers Press
published by arrangement with
Peter MacTaggert

ISBN 0 7540 8616 X

Copyright © 1955 by Peter MacTaggert

British Library Cataloguing in Publication Data available

Printed and bound in Great Britain by
Bookcraft, Midsomer Norton, Somerset

CHAPTER ONE

THE FAINT TINKLE of the shop-bell interrupted Fanny Lynam in her attempt to think clearly about the coming week-end. Muttering annoyance, she levered her heavy body out of a deep armchair. Martin, the cat, dislodged without warning from her lap, slithered to the floor, mewing resentment. His yellow eyes followed her suspiciously as she went to the door, while Spike, the dog, lifting his head from the hearthrug, gave a drowsy yelp in formal recognition of the presence of strangers.

Fanny did not hurry, but paused by the table to stub out her cigarette and again before a mirror to fumble for a moment with her short, rough, greying hair. The mirror, framed in gilt, was old and precious, and Fanny's face, reflected in the flawed and sombre depths of the glass, was robbed of its florid colour; her short-sighted eyes had a blank, fierce stare and her full, firm chin looked long and hollow. This view of herself did not disturb her.

As she went slowly down the passage to the shop, her loose felt slippers slapped on the stone floor. She was wearing slacks that had fitted her two years before, but which no longer buttoned comfortably at the waist. Above them she wore a shapeless sweater, knitted by herself for her second husband, Basil Lynam, who had not protested when she had decided to borrow it back from him. Round the high collar of the sweater she wore a fine Victorian necklace of seed-pearls. She was a shortish woman, fifty years old, lethargic in her movements and at the moment vague and self-absorbed in manner.

" Good morning," she said automatically as she entered the shop.

It was full of sunshine. It streamed in through the one narrow window that overlooked the village street and showed up the film of dust on the polished surfaces of table and tall-

5

boy, bureau and carved chest. The air was full of moving specks of dust.

The customer, a woman in a fur coat and small hat, had taken a pewter tankard from a shelf and was turning it round in her gloved hands.

Going forward with her saleswoman's smile, Fanny said, " Yes, that mug's nice, isn't it? You've picked the good one. The other two are reproductions."

" How much is it? " the woman asked.

" I think it's thirty shillings. May I take a look? . . . Yes, thirty shillings," Fanny said. " It's part of a set really, but I've been selling them separately."

" It's got initials on it," the woman said. " I'd prefer it without initials."

" You can easily have them taken off," Fanny said. " I could get it done for you in two or three days for about five shillings."

" I shan't be here for two or three days, I'm just driving through," the woman said.

" I could send it after you."

" Oh no, thank you, I don't think I want to bother. How much is that little china jug over there? "

This was the question, Fanny knew, that the woman had come into the shop to ask.

" Oh, that—I'm afraid that's rather expensive," Fanny said. " It's genuine Chelsea."

" How much? "

" Six pounds."

The woman gave a startled laugh, asked the price of one or two other knick-knacks, remarked what a beautiful day it was for the time of year, and left.

Fanny, who had not expected to make a sale and whose thoughts had barely left the subject with which they had been busy all the morning, turned and went back along the stone-flagged passage to the sitting-room.

It was a big room with a low ceiling and with most of one wall taken up by a great fireplace. Logs were stacked there, ready for lighting, but just then the room was warmed only by an electric fire. This was set close to the chair in which

Fanny had been sitting and which Martin the cat had now adopted for himself. Most of the stone floor was covered by a deep grey carpet. There were several easy-chairs, a long bookcase, some old prints of birds and flowers and the gilt-framed mirror.

As usual, in passing the mirror, Fanny cast a glance at the strange, drowned face that gazed back at her as out of a shadowed pool. Then she crossed the room to the deep embrasure framing one of the small windows and stood looking intently down at a photograph that stood on the sill, next to a Spode bowl full of daffodils. The photograph had been standing there for three days, but Fanny had still not made up her mind what she thought about it.

For what did a photograph tell you at the best of times? A photograph could lie with far more authority, could per-petuate a far more impenetrable deception than any painting.

Luckily, perhaps, Fanny had to make a telephone call that morning to her friend, Clare Forwood, and so could not spend much more time staring at the photograph, asking herself unanswerable questions about it. She had meant to telephone Clare immediately after breakfast, but then had slipped into a spell of musing and chain-smoking and it had been a shock, when the shop-bell roused her, to realise how late it was. Turning now from the window with an uneasy sigh, she jolted Martin out of the chair, sat down and reached first for a cigarette, then for the telephone.

She gave Clare's Hampstead number. While she waited, the cat, purring noisily, sprang on to her knees and started to turn round and round there, seeking for perfect comfort. In a mood of irritation, Fanny pushed him off. She avoided looking towards the window and the photograph, but picking up a pencil and old envelope, started drawing squares and circles.

Presently a voice spoke remotely in her ear. It sounded impatient, because Clare Forwood hated being rung up during the morning, when she was writing.

Fanny said, " About that man Poulter, Clare . . ."

The impatience vanished from Clare Forwood's voice. " Yes ? " she said quickly.

" I've fixed it for you," Fanny said. " He's coming to cocktails on Saturday.   So all you have to do, if you still want
to meet him, is come down for the week-end."

" How did you work it? " Clare asked.

" He walked into the shop yesterday," Fanny said. " He
bought a rather horrible corner-cupboard I've had on my
hands two years.   Then he stayed on talking.   He wanted
advice on woodworm, he said.   And one thing led to another
till I took the plunge and simply invited him.   He seemed
very pleased, so I think it must have been what he wanted.
Can you manage next week-end? "

" Oh yes.   And thanks, Fanny, thanks very much.   Though
I almost feel . . ." Clare's voice had changed again, sounding
hesitant and guarded.   " I've been thinking it over since I
told you I'd like to meet him, and really it seems rather
stupid.   I'm so bad at meeting strange people."

" You mean you *don't* want to meet him now? " Fanny
asked.

" Oh, I do," Clare said, " but when it actually comes to
the point, I'm afraid I'll—well, you know what I'm like."

" Look," Fanny said, " I only asked him because you
wanted me to."

" Yes, I know.   But I suppose I never seriously expected
you to do anything about it."

" And there's something I want you to do for me in return,"
Fanny went on firmly, " so for heaven's sake don't walk out
on it now.   Kit's gone and got himself engaged.   I haven't
met the girl yet—I've only got her photograph—but she's
coming down next week-end.   Well, will you pick her up and
drive her down with you? "

" I see," Clare said and was silent for a moment.   " All
right," she said.   " But tell me, Fanny, did you tell Poulter
that I'd be there or say anything about my specially wanting
to meet him? "

" Not a thing."

" So if I don't feel like it, I needn't even talk to him? "

" You needn't say a word."

" Good.   Who is the girl, Fanny? "

" Her name's Laura Greenslade.   She's a journalist.   Among

other things, she does scientific bits for lots of papers and
Basil says that, all considered, they aren't too bad. The
funny thing is, she was a student of his once. He remembered
her as soon as he heard her name, though he doesn't seem
able to remember much else about her, except that he thinks
there was something or other peculiar about her. Being
Basil, that might mean she'd murdered her grandmother or
that she could waggle her ears, the second being rather the
more interesting. But the really peculiar thing, in my view,
is her wanting to marry Kit. She's extraordinarily beautiful—to judge by her photograph—she's clever and she's
making a good income. And none of that can be said about
Kit."

" You sound a bit worried," Clare said. " Are you? "

" Oh no, I'm not, I'm glad, I'm really delighted," Fanny
said. " It's time Kit got married. And I've been planning
how to convert the house so that they can have part of it
completely to themselves. Fortunately, having once been
two cottages, it'll be quite easy to make it into two again.
The only trouble is, a half is going to be a little small for
them, as there's a child. She's been married before. Her
husband was killed in the war and the child's been living
with Laura's mother, but of course she'll want to have her
here once she's married and got a proper home."

" I see," Clare said.

" Why do you say ' I see,' like that? " Fanny asked.

" How did I say it? "

" Significantly."

" I didn't mean to. But I still think you sound worried."

" Naturally I'm very nervous," Fanny said. " That's
partly why I'm anxious to have you here this week-end.
You may be bad at meeting people, but you're quite good
sometimes at summing them up, and if you have her with
you when you drive down you'll really have a chance to find
out what you think about her."

" What difference will it make what either of us think
about her? "

Fanny jabbed her cigarette at the ash-tray with a small,
fierce gesture.

" None at all, of course," she said.   " But I'd still like to
know what you think.   That's natural, isn't it? "

" When d'you want us to arrive? " Clare asked.

" Can you manage lunch-time on Saturday? . . . Good.
I'll expect you around one.   And don't worry about meeting
the Poulter man, Clare.   He seemed to be a very mild old
thing.   You'd never think he'd ever owned a string of newspapers."

Fanny rang off.   Martin the cat, taking this as a propitious
sign, jumped up on to her lap again and this time was allowed
to remain.   One of Fanny's hands started to slide softly
over the smooth fur of his back.   The other hand, having
got rid of her cigarette, went on absently drawing squares
and circles on the old envelope.   Then presently she began to
write on it.   She wrote: " Stuffed olives.   Salted almonds.
Cheese straws.   Sausages.   Anchovies.   Biscuits.   Lobster. . . ."

She paused there, looking fixedly at what she had written,
then she underlined the word " lobster " several times.

At that point she was interrupted by the opening of the
door.   It was Kit Raven, her half-brother, who came into
the room.

Kit was twenty years younger than Fanny.   His mother,
dead many years before, had been only twenty-three when
she had married Fanny's father.   She had been a stolid, good-
natured girl who had always treated Fanny with affection,
though she had worried continually over what she had considered the wild and disorderly life led by Fanny before and
during her first marriage.   On her death, only two years
after that of her elderly husband, Fanny had been almost
surprised at the strength of her grief for her stepmother, and,
rather wryly, she sometimes said now that if Christine had
lived to see it, she would have been more than delighted at
the change that had come over her on her marriage to Basil
Lynam.   That Fanny would give up the stage, live in the
country, grow fat, keep a dog and a cat, sell antiques and
join the Women's Institute, was something that Christine
would never have believed possible.

Kit Raven, at thirty, was a stockily-built, wide-shouldered
young man of medium height, with long, heavily-muscled

arms and big, square-palmed craftsman's hands. His hair was yellow, his eyes were a cheerful blue, his skin was ruddy. A fullness about the cheeks and a heaviness about the chin, which gave his face a certain resemblance to his sister's, suggested that later, like her, he would put on weight, but for the present his waist was still slender and his walk light and quick. There was good nature in his face and a look of common sense and humour. Only occasionally the blue eyes betrayed confusion and a deep self-distrust. If he was not handsome, he was, as Fanny had learnt many years earlier, very attractive to women.

"Hallo," he said, picking up the envelope from the arm of Fanny's chair, and reading what she had written. "Making plans for the party?"

"Yes, and I thought you might order the things for me this morning," she said.

"I haven't time for that," he said. "I've got to get over to that sale at Chedbury."

"This would only take a few minutes."

Kit hated to be involved in domestic matters.

"You haven't written down how much you want of anything," he said. "I shouldn't have the faintest idea what to order. And lobster—you're going to make your lobster thingummies, are you? Will you want it fresh or tinned?"

"Fresh, of course," Fanny said.

"Well, I haven't the faintest idea how to buy lobster, except in tins," Kit said, handing the envelope back. "There's no hurry, anyway. You've got half the week. Who's coming?"

"The man Poulter."

"I know. And Clare?"

"Yes, though she seemed to get scared when I told her I'd actually fixed it."

"Why d'you suppose she's so keen to meet him?" Kit asked curiously. "D'you think she wants to persuade him to give her a job on one of his papers?"

"Good God, no!" Fanny said. "All Clare will ever do is write the same story about her own fantastic family over and over again, getting more and more obscure and distinguished as time goes on."

"But suppose she's short of money," Kit said. "Those books can't bring in much."

"More than you'd think," Fanny said. "But if she were short of money, which I'm sure she isn't, she'd drown herself before she thought of journalism."

"Then why does she want to meet Poulter?"

"One can never guess Clare's reasons. But at least she's going to drive Laura down in the morning, so you'd better write to Laura and tell her so."

"Fine," Kit said. "Whom else have you asked?"

"No one, yet. But I'm going to ask the Gregorys, of course, and probably the McLeans and—and perhaps the Mordues." Over the last name she hesitated for an instant.

Kit frowned a little.

"If you ask old Mordue, nobody else will come," he said.

"I know. It's difficult, isn't it? But I can't help asking them, can I?" Fanny's gaze rested again on the photograph of Laura Greenslade, shadowed by the yellow trumpets of the daffodils, while her hand slid along the soft, coiled body of the cat. "I'm rather fond of the old devil myself, even if no one else can stand him, and I like Minnie—and Susan— very much."

"Minnie's so damned woebegone and sorry for herself," Kit said. "Have we really got to ask them?"

"She may be awfully hurt if we don't," Fanny said. "So may Susan."

"Hell!" He turned to the door. "Well, do what you think best."

"Kit——" she said quickly.

He did not turn to face her, though he stood still. His wide shoulders were a little hunched, his rather thick neck was somewhat sunk between them. It was the attitude of someone extremely on the defensive.

Fanny went on, "Tom and Minnie aren't the reason why you don't want me to ask them, are they?"

"I told you," he answered in a sullen tone, "do what you think best."

" If I invite them and tell them——"

" Tell them what? " he demanded sharply as she paused.

" Oh, that the Poulter man's coming and Clare and Laura and all, then they can come or not as they choose and at least Minnie can't think I want to drop them, as so many other people have done."

" If Tom knows Poulter's going to be here, he'll insist on coming, then pick a quarrel with him when he gets here," Kit said. " But do what you like. It doesn't matter to me."

He went out.

Thrusting her fingers through her hair, Fanny gave a harsh sigh, then reached once more for the telephone.

First she rang up her next-door neighbours, the Gregorys, but both Jean and Colin were out. Next she rang up Mrs. McLean, the wife of the local doctor. Mrs. McLean said that she would be delighted to meet Kit's fiancée, then talked for twenty minutes about the flowers that the last two days of sunshine had brought out in her garden. She was the most overpowering garden-lover in the village and once started could remain on the subject for hours at a time. But at last she rang off. With a good deal of reluctance, Fanny dialled the Mordues' number.

Her ring was answered by Minnie Mordue, as Fanny had known it would be, for at that hour Susan was always out at work and Tom never answered the telephone at any hour, but only shouted curses at it for ringing, followed sometimes by curses at Minnie, if she made a mistake in any message she brought him.

Tom was a retired schoolmaster with a very small pension, who lived in a cottage about three miles out of the village. The cottage had no conveniences of any kind and Minnie, a shaggy-haired, sad-eyed woman with boundless physical energy but a drained and exhausted spirit, did all the laborious work of the household, without any help from her husband, even in chopping firewood or carrying coal. But though she complained about this constantly, in her heart she never really questioned its rightness, and when she saw Basil Lynam, who, as a university lecturer, impressed her as

being even higher in the scale of intellectual eminence than
Tom, doing the washing-up, marketing and sometimes even
cooking, she felt that Fanny was blameworthy and deserved
to lose the love of her husband. Yet she was very fond of
Fanny, who had contrived, over several years, to remain
amused at Tom's quarrelsomeness and so had been allowed
by him to remain a friend of Minnie's.

To-day, however, when Fanny invited her and her family
to the cocktail party on Saturday, Minnie was evasive. She
said that she must consult Tom, and, of course, Susan too,
before she could accept.

This was what Fanny had expected, but it depressed her.
Wearily, she said that if she found that they could not come,
she would of course understand.

Minnie seemed to grasp at this thankfully.

" I know, dear," she said, " I know you will. And that's
such a blessing, not having to explain. And perhaps we will
come—I'd love to, of course—but if Susan should feel . . .
Well, you know what she's like. She's very reserved and so
I simply don't know what she's really feeling at the minute.
But I'd hate to make her do anything that . . . Well, you
know what I mean, so I won't go into it. This girl, this
Miss Greenslade——"

" Mrs. Greenslade," Fanny said. " She's a widow."

" Well, this Mrs. Greenslade, you do like her, don't you,
dear? You do think Kit will be happy with her? "

" I haven't met her yet," Fanny said. " At least Kit
seems to be very much in love with her."

" Good, good," Minnie said in a voice that shook a little.
" Marriage will be the making of him. Well, thanks for the
invitation, dear. I'll ring you up and tell you if we can come
when I've consulted Tom—and, of course, Susan. Give Kit
our love, won't you? And be sure to tell him that we all hope
he'll be very happy."

Fanny put the telephone down, then took one more long
look across the room at the photograph of Laura Greenslade.

Yes, beautiful, she told herself, and intelligent—but what
else?

Pushing the cat off her lap, she got up, pocketed the envelope on which she had written down her requirements for the party and crossed to the door.

Taking an old coat off a peg in the passage, she kicked off her slippers and stepped into a pair of gumboots, then went down the passage, through the shop and out into the street, releasing the catch of the shop door as she did so and turning a card that hung on the door, so that, seen from outside, it read, " Back presently." ·

There was, of course, no need for her to order immediately most of the things that she had written down on the envelope, but talking to Minnie, holding in half the things that she had really wanted to say, had left her restless. Besides, it would be a good idea to have a talk with Harris, the combined greengrocer and fishmonger, about a lobster.

•

CHAPTER TWO

As FANNY reached the street, Tom Mordue, in the bar of The Waggoners, was saying in his high, harsh voice, which could always be heard over any other voices in the room, " You're asking me what I think about it, Mr. Davin? You want to know what *I* think? Well then, I'll tell you, but don't blame me if you don't like it, because I never bother to falsify my opinions. Life isn't long enough for that. Sometimes I keep my opinions to myself, but when I give them, I give them like an honest man. And you *asked* me what I think. Well then, what I think is that you're a gullible fool, Mr. Davin. Just that. A gullible fool, like ninety-nine per cent of the people in this country—or any other country. Yes, a gullible fool, sir, on whom an education at the country's expense has been completely wasted, since apparently it hasn't taught you even the elements of clear thinking. Nearly all education is completely wasted, as no one knows better than I. If I had my way, I'd abolish it. All of it. Back to illiteracy, Mr. Davin, since then at least people like yourself would be saved from exploitation by every fake and phoney who thinks up some pretentious formula which he can afford to have printed and with which he imposes on your credulity."

"Hold hard, Tom," Colin Gregory muttered in Tom Mordue's ear. "If you go on like that, there'll be trouble."

"Trouble?" Tom Mordue said as loudly as before. "The man asked me for my opinion, didn't he? I was sitting here quietly drinking my beer and he disturbed my thoughts to ask me my opinion about a ridiculous patent medicine which he claims relieved his lumbago. Well, what d'you expect me to reply? D'you think I should congratulate him and advise him to go on throwing his hard-earned money away on bottle after bottle of worthless coloured water? No, I'm not that sort, my boy. I never thrust my opinions on anybody——"

Someone in the bar drew in a derisive breath.

"I *never*," Tom Mordue repeated, "force my opinions on anybody, but when I'm asked for them, I give them openly, sincerely and without fear or favour."

"But with a bloody lot of unnecessary insults," Fred Davin growled, getting off his stool and walking to the door. He was an elderly, thick-set, slow-moving man, who kept the local ironmonger's shop and was widely known for a curious and almost total inability to send out bills to his customers. Most of them being honest people, they would often almost implore him to be allowed to pay what they owed, but that for Fred Davin would have meant days and nights of struggle with ledgers and accounts and would greatly have interfered with the time he spent in The Waggoners.

"That stuff did me good, he said." Turning in the doorway, he stared at Tom Mordue and made his declaration of faith. "It cured my lumbago in three days, and that's more than ever happened with anything Dr. McLean gave me, though I've got nothing against him, he's a good man and he does his best. But that stuff cured my lumbago in three days."

He went out.

"Shame on you, Mr. Mordue," said Mrs. Toles from behind the bar. "If that had been anyone but Fred Davin you said those things to we'd have had a scene. But you can

tell what he felt, because that's the first time I've known Fred
Davin leave before closing-time for a good couple of years."

" And if he'd do that a bit more often, it'd do his lumbago
a lot more good than all his patent medicines," Tom Mordue
said.

" Pipe down, Tom," Colin Gregory said. " It doesn't
amuse people."

Tom Mordue's reply was a high cackle of laughter.

He was a small, wrinkled, red-faced man, with a large head
that was almost entirely bald and with thick, white eyebrows
over small, keen, restless eyes. His mouth was almost lipless
and opened, when he laughed, to show great, clumsy false
teeth. He always sat stiffly upright, but he could never keep
quite still and was always jigging with one foot or twisting
his fingers round one another.

After a moment he said, " You're my only friend, Colin—
you and Fanny Lynam, that's to say. I love Fanny, God
bless her." He raised his beer mug in salute to her and
drank.

" But what makes you do it, Tom? " Colin Gregory asked.
" If the old boy thinks his mixture did him some good, why
not let him go on thinking it? Then it'll probably go on
doing him good."

" I can't stand self-deception, Colin," Tom Mordue
answered. " I can't stand pretences and hypocrisy. It's no
good asking me to. I know my life would have been far
more comfortable if I'd been able to make myself do it.
I might have been rich, popular, sought after. But there are
some things a man can't control. They go against his nature
and there's nothing he can do about it."

" It goes against your nature to pass up a chance for a
row," Colin said.

He was a tall, slim, indolent-looking man of thirty-three,
with a narrow, rather handsome, sunburnt face, wide, stooping
shoulders, reserved grey eyes, and a lazy, good-humoured
smile. He was sitting now with his long legs crossed, a pipe
in his mouth and a pint of beer on the table in front of him.
Nearby a big log-fire burnt on an open hearth. There was a
fox's mask on the wall above the fireplace and a badger's

above the door. Pewter pots hung in a row from a shelf.
There were half a dozen other people in the bar.

Tom Mordue, keeping his restless eyes on them, as if
he were watching for another possible point of attack, found
their ranks closed against him. Their backs were turned
towards him and their voices were lowered. There was no
show of antagonism, but merely a placid impenetrability.

As if this had suddenly become more than he could bear,
he got off his stool and muttering to Colin Gregory, " Well,
see you to-morrow, Colin," he walked to the door.

He had a rapid, jerky walk with his shoulders thrown
back and his arms held stiffly at his sides without swinging
at all.

At the door he called out, " Good morning," and was
answered with polite good mornings from most of the people
there.

Emerging into the sunshine of the street, he set off briskly
along it, at first looking a little doubtful of himself but soon
recovering his usual air of defiant self-satisfaction. He just
missed meeting Fanny Lynam, who, a moment after Tom
had passed, came out of Harris's, having ordered the lobster
that she wanted for her party, and went towards The
Waggoners.

Going inside and finding Colin she subsided with a sigh
on the settle beside him and let a variety of parcels drop on
to the table in front of her.

" I thought I might find you here," she said. " I rang up
your house and that passionately protective housekeeper of
yours wouldn't drop a hint as to your probable whereabouts,
so I thought I could make a pretty good guess where I'd
find you. Where's Jean? "

" At some committee meeting," Colin said. " What'll you
have to drink? "

" Gin and tonic, please."

He gave the order, then told her, " You've just missed
something here."

" Tom out for trouble as usual? "

" Got it in one."

Fanny lit a cigarette. Her manner was absent-minded.

"It's awful, isn't it? D'you think he's been as bad as this all his life, or is it the effect retirement's had on him?"

"I should think he's always been pretty bad," Colin said. "But he used to have a lot of little boys to take it out on and little boys take such a poor view of human nature anyway that they may have tolerated him better than we do."

"You and I tolerate him remarkably well," Fanny said. "I do it because I'm sorry for Minnie and you do it because you can't be bothered not to."

"And anyway, we both quite like the old devil, in spite of ourselves—possibly because he brings some diversion into our quiet lives." Colin passed up his mug for more beer. "Actually I think he's got worse lately. He seems to be—well, nervous."

"I know, I know." Fanny's tone was defensive, as if he had made an accusation of some sort.

Colin caught that note and said, "Never mind, my dear. There's nothing you can do about it."

"But it makes it all the more difficult about my party on Saturday," she said. "With both him and Minnie being so extra touchy at the moment, I feel I'll probably give offence whatever I do."

"What party is this?" Colin asked. "Am I invited?"

"Yes, of course—you and Jean. That's why I was trying to track you down. Cocktails on Saturday. Kit's young woman is coming for the week-end and she's so beautiful and so brilliant that I feel I need all the moral support I can get."

"Kit's young woman?" Colin's thoughtful eyes dwelt for a moment on Fanny's rather flushed face. "The lovely in the photograph on your window-sill?"

"Yes—Laura Greenslade—Mrs. Greenslade, widow, with one child," Fanny said. "Can you imagine Kit a step-father?"

"Why not?"

"Well, he's so young, so . . . well, not really so young, of course, but unformed, isn't he?"

"I hadn't noticed it particularly," Colin said.

" Perhaps I'm prejudiced. It's easy to be prejudiced about one's own family. But you and Jean will come, won't you? "

" I wouldn't miss it for anything."

" I've collected Sir Peter Poulter," Fanny said in a satisfied tone. " That ought to impress her. And Clare Forwood's driving her down, so she'll see that she's marrying into a very distinguished circle."

" Won't she just! " His tone was amused but no smile came into his grey eyes. " Why does she have to be impressed, Fanny? What's the matter with her? "

Fanny flicked cigarette ash on to the floor. She avoided his gaze.

" I'm sure there's nothing the matter with her," she said. " Basil, who used to know her a little, says there was something peculiar about her, but I'm sure that doesn't mean anything. No, I'm sure she's a charming, intelligent, nice-natured girl and that we're all going to love her. The only thing is . . ."

" Well? "

" Well, damn it, Colin, what does someone as charming, intelligent and so on as all that want with my poor Kit? "

" Kit's very attractive—you ought to know that by now," he said.

" Yes, but to *marry* . . ."

Colin burst out laughing.

Fanny did not respond but sat frowning at the drink in front of her. Instead of helping to cheer her up, it was making the depression, which had weighed on her mind for the last day or two, start getting out of hand. But she did not want to let Colin, or anyone else, see any sign of it. She was pleased about Kit's engagement, so she had told Kit, Basil, her friends and most forcibly of all, herself. She was determined to remain pleased at all costs. Fingering her glass, still frowning at it distantly, she said, " The trouble with me at the moment is stage fright. Know what I mean, Colin? "

" Of course," he answered. " It's quite natural too."

" But it isn't a thing I suffer from much as a rule. Perhaps I'd have been a better actress if I'd had more of it—that's what they tell you. But I always just enjoyed myself on the stage. Only that seems a long time ago now and I've altered a lot since then. I couldn't go back to that life now for anything."

She paused. She did not really know what she was trying to say to Colin, but for some reason she always tended to say more to him than she intended.

This happened without his apparently doing anything to encourage it. She thought it must be because he was really much more like the people among whom she had spent most of her life than anyone else among her present friends and neighbours. It was easy to imagine Colin an actor, a not very talented actor, able to live reasonably comfortably, however, on his looks and the earnings of a hard-working, devoted wife. That had been the pattern of Fanny's first marriage. Now the thought of that time and the way that she had wasted all the passion of her youth on a worthless man when there were others like Basil Lynam in the world filled her with a kind of rage. Yet it was a disconcerting fact that when she had had a drink or two she always found it so easy to talk too much to Colin Gregory.

Not that he was really in the least like her first husband, except in the one respect, that he apparently saw no objection to letting his wife keep him. But it was not only on Jean's dividends that he depended for his pleasant existence, not on her hard work at a time when she might have been having children. Jean had a child and Colin, Fanny felt certain, adored both the child and Jean. And since he was lucky enough to be married to one of the few people left in this difficult world who had plenty of money, there was no reason that Fanny could see why he should not enjoy his good fortune in his own way.

" Stage fright," Fanny repeated. " Because she's beautiful and smart and belongs to that world that I couldn't keep up with any longer."

" Or grew out of," Colin suggested.

She gave him a bright smile. " You're such a comfort, Colin. But d'you know, there's something I sometimes wonder about ? . . . About Basil. You see, he thought he was marrying an actress. I weighed eight stone three, had my hair done properly every week, always wore high heels and paid the earth, as a matter of course, for black-market nylons. Now my weight's nearly eleven stone, I cut my own hair as often as not, go about in gumboots and . . . well, look, suppose Basil really wanted those other things. D'you see what I mean? Suppose, just because he's such a quiet, intellectual sort of person, those other things really had an awful lot of glamour for him, so that I've really let him down terribly badly. . . ."

" My guess is," Colin said, " that Basil never thinks of criticising a single thing you do."

" But suppose . . ."

" Have another drink," Colin said, " and cheer up. You've got the great Sir Peter coming to your party, and Clare Forwood——"

" Yes, and I'm going to make my special lobster patties," Fanny said, " which are almost the only thing I know how to make well. I'm a lousy cook, but I do know how to make those."

" So everything's bound to be a tremendous success and you've nothing whatever to worry about."

" But I'm not worrying about the *party*, Colin."

" I know," he said. " It's Laura—going on and on. But it had to happen some time, my dear. Kit's a marrying sort of man."

" Sometimes you're just too full of homely wisdom for words! " Fanny said, her face darkening with a flash of bad temper. " Of course it had to happen some time—but why in hell did it have to go and happen with a Laura Greenslade? "

" That's just fate. You can't escape fate." With an unusual touch of grimness, he added, " None of us can."

Fanny began to gather up her parcels.

" Well, tell Jean about the party," she said. " And I'll see you on Saturday, if not before."

Colin nodded with a good-humoured look of understanding.

Fanny got up and went out into the street.

The spring sunshine had a growing warmth in it and she paused just outside the door to feel the pleasantness on her face. There were no signs of green yet on the trees, but there were jonquils, grape hyacinths and crocuses in the cottage gardens. Just why she had become angry with Colin at just that moment, she did not know and now she did not want to think about it. So after a moment she started to walk along quickly, clutching her parcels to her with both arms, humming a tune, while her gumboots thudded softly on the grass verge of the street. It was wide, with two rows of elms along it. Set far back behind the trees, the houses, for the most part, were Queen Anne or older, with only one or two Victorian interruptions in the general charm of age. The village was a famous one, much visited in the summer by tourists.

The real trouble, Fanny thought as she walked along, the thing that she could not face, was that Laura meant change. That was funny, when you came to think of it, because once upon a time perpetual change had been the only thing that had made life endurable.

At the garden gate she met Minnie Mordue.

Minnie had been knocking at the door, and receiving no answer, had been just about to come away when, seeing Fanny, she had halted.

As Fanny came up to her, Minnie clutched eagerly at one of her arms so that several parcels fell to the ground.

" I've hardly got a minute, dear," Minnie said in her hurried breathless way, " but I must just come in and tell you. . . ." She was stooping to rescue the parcels as she spoke. " Tom's waiting for me to drive him home, you see, so I mustn't stay, but I did want to tell you. . . . Not that I've really anything to tell you, till I've spoken to Susan this evening, but at least Tom thinks there isn't any reason why we shouldn't come to the party on Saturday."

Carrying the dropped parcels, she was trotting up the path behind Fanny. She was a tall, ungainly woman, only a year or two older than Fanny, but with a drained and faded elderly quality that made Fanny's florid stoutness look like the well-being of youth. She had limp, shoulder-length grey hair and large, anxious, hazel eyes, always ringed with blue, so that, in spite of an extraordinary fund of physical energy, she looked as if she were in a continual state of exhaustion. Her

clothes were shapeless, home-made and everlasting. She
always carried a large leather bag, filled with mysterious
pieces of paper, in which she had to rummage for minutes
at a time to find such things as a comb, a handkerchief or
money.

Following Fanny into the sitting-room, she sat down on
the edge of a chair, repeating that she could only stay a
minute. Fanny was accustomed, however, to a breathless air
of transitoriness in Minnie and knew that in fact she might
easily stay an hour. She at least had time this morning to
have her usual conversation with Spike, a bull terrier with a
touch of spaniel about him, who liked to rest his chin on her
knee, gazing up at her intimately while she murmured com-
pliments to him on his nature and appearance.

But her voice, as she did this to-day, had a deep sadness
in it, as if she could not help a regretful comparison between
his excellent qualities and some less satisfactory in certain
human beings. It was a tone that played havoc with Fanny's
nerves. It felt like an accusation, a back-handed attack on
herself. Suddenly, almost angrily, she exclaimed, " Well, it
wasn't my fault, Minnie! I'm as upset as you are. I always
hoped, just as much as you did, that Kit and Susan would
marry, but that isn't the kind of thing one can arrange for
other people."

" But Susan . . . Susan's so unhappy! " There was an
unfamiliar wildness in Minnie's voice. " I'm sure she is,
I'm sure she's really in love with the boy, Fanny, and I
think she was quite sure he was in love with her. Of course
I wouldn't say that to anyone but you."

" I should hope not, for Susan's sake! "

" Of course I wouldn't. But still, Fanny, it's so terrible
seeing her determined to smile it off and saying she's longing
to meet this Mrs. Greenslade and hoping that Kit will be
very happy. Fanny dear, I'm very fond of that boy, and I
suppose in my heart I know I can't blame him, because
that's the way things happen and there's nothing one can
do about it, but all the same, just at the minute . . ." Her
big, worn hands had gone on fondling Spike's flopping spaniel
ears, but now, for a moment, the long fingers changed

into talons, threatening the dog. Startled, he jerked his head away from her. " Still, that wouldn't help my Susan, would it? " she said. " But that's why I'm not sure about Saturday."

Fanny nodded. " I know."

" Tom thinks we ought to come," Minnie went on. " He thinks Susan will want to. I think perhaps she will too, because she's very proud and she'll want to show people that she isn't really hurt. But I'm not sure that she ought to make herself go through a thing like that." She looked across the room at the photograph on the window-sill. " That's Laura, is it? "

Fanny nodded again.

The two women went on looking thoughtfully at the photograph.

After a minute, Minnie said, " Well, if it's a good likeness, she's very lovely and I can quite understand Kit falling in love with her, but to my mind there's something peculiar about that face, though I can't say just what it is that strikes me like that."

" Peculiar? " Fanny's voice was shrill.

" Don't you see it? " Minnie asked interestedly. " Doesn't it strike you too? I thought you told me——"

" That was Basil," Fanny said. " I don't see anything peculiar about her at all. I don't. I think—I think she just looks beautiful and charming and intelligent! "

CHAPTER THREE

JEAN GREGORY, walking home after a meeting of the Church Restoration Fund Committee, which had occupied nearly the whole of her morning, met her husband as he came out of The Waggoners.

Jean was a fragile-looking woman of thirty. She had a small and finely modelled head, carried high between narrow and rather sloping shoulders. Her features were small and regular, her skin was delicate and perfect. She had brown, softly curling hair, which was cut very short, and large brown eyes, emotional and serious.   There was always an air of intensity and faint austerity about her, a suggestion, almost, of the nun.

This was often heightened, as it was to-day, by the way she was dressed.   A grey coat, buttoned up to her neck, with a small, round collar, swung loose from her shoulders; her long, slim-fingered hands were invisible, buried deep in her pockets; her shoes were black and flat-heeled.

Meeting Colin, she slipped her arm through his and as they walked towards their home, she started to tell him about the committee meeting.

Usually it amused him to hear her accounts of her activities in the village.   She described them with self-deprecating flippancy, though they were really of the deepest importance to her.   She was a very shy woman and her conscience never left her in peace because she was rich.   Colin often mocked her for this, but fortunately for them both, since she was really very easily hurt, he had a sensitive touch and seldom said the word that went too far.   In fact, she usually enjoyed his mockery, feeling that it helped her to remember the extreme insignificance of herself and her works.

To-day, however, he was not mocking.   He appeared not to be in the least amused and after a few minutes it dawned on Jean that he was not even interested.   His face, when she considered it, was unusually abstracted.

She waited for a little, then asked, " What's the matter, Colin? "

" The Mordues," he answered at once.

" Oh dear," she said.   " Because of this engagement of Kit's? "

" Yes.   Tom's so cut up, he's becoming quite unbearable. He tried hard to pick a quarrel with Fred Davin to-day."

" Tom worships Susan," Jean said in extenuation.

" I know, heaven help the girl," Colin said.   " If he'd give a little more worship to poor, down-trodden Minnie and let Susan run her own affairs——"

" But he does worship Minnie, you know."

" Queer form it takes, then."

" I expect nearly all real worship takes queer forms."

He gave a curious glance at her small, earnest face.

" Well, he can have Minnie, so far as I'm concerned," he said, " but I wish Susan could be rescued."

" But, Colin, what's come over you? " She acted extreme surprise. " Don't you always argue that there's nothing one can do about other people, that they make their own fates and the only thing is to let them get ahead with the job? "

" Do I? " His eyes had their most reserved look, a look that had often made Jean feel that behind his good humour and his liking for pleasing other people, there might be qualities of which she had no knowledge. " It's more or less what I've been saying to Fanny," he admitted, " to try and cheer her up. She hates this engagement almost as much as Tom does, though that's only partly on account of Susan. Still, at the moment I feel that if someone could persuade Susan to go a long way off before the lovely Mrs. Greenslade settles here and Susan slips into the habit of being an object of pity, they'd be doing a very kindly act."

" But she's got her job," Jean said uncertainly. " And I think she's fond of those children she looks after."

" There must be lots of children in other places who need looking after. As a matter of fact, I was thinking——"

" You were thinking of Joe and Miriam! " Jean exclaimed.

" As a matter of fact, I was," Colin said. " Don't they need a nurse quite badly? "

" They did—though they may have found one by now," Jean said. " At any rate, you could ring up and ask. That might be doing a good turn to everybody."

" Wouldn't that be nice for a change? "

" It's a new strain coming out in you. But tell me more about Fanny, Colin. What's wrong with the engagement from her point of view? I thought she seemed quite pleased and excited when she told me about it."

" Intermittently, I expect, she is," he said. " But then she gets so wild with jealousy, she's ready to hate the girl. By the way, we're invited to cocktails on Saturday."

" To meet Laura? "

" And Clare Forwood and Sir Peter Poulter."

She gave him a startled look. He nodded. Jean frowned unhappily.

" That does sound rather like jealousy or something," she said. " I mean, trying so hard to impress—though Clare Forwood, of course, is a very old friend and it's quite natural to ask her in the circumstances."

" But you feel that laying on Sir Peter Poulter too is going a bit far? "

" No, of course not. Not exactly. But . . ."

He patted her hand. " Fanny herself thinks so. She told me all about it."

" About being jealous too? "

" In a way. If Fanny gives herself away unintentionally, she generally catches up on it in time to turn the lapse into charming candour. Only she wanted me to think that she was jealous of Basil, rather than of Kit. She feels that's more normal."

Jean looked at him seriously, questioningly, then reluctantly she smiled.

" You *are* an awful cat, of course," she said.

" It's how I while away my idle life."

They had reached their gate. With his hand upon it to push it open, Colin stood still. For a moment his eyes searched hers.

" Jean," he said, " Jean darling, you do hate my idle life, don't you? "

" No," she said. " Don't start that now. Please."

She walked quickly up the path ahead of him.

Their house, next door to the Lynams', was not as old. Its Georgian brick looked almost modern beside the other. The spring sunshine, entering through tall sash windows, fell on white-painted panelling and lovingly polished mahogany. It was a sedate house, that looked as if it had always been lived in calmly and with an attitude of reserve. It was without the strange shadows and general unexpectedness of the house next door. For all its sunniness, there was some severity about it. It demanded a certain standard of its inhabitants.

To Jean this was as it should be. She had something here

to live up to, something that mere money, that terrible
liability which kept her permanently in debt to life, could
not supply. Here it was essential to have taste and a sense of
fitness. Jean would never have felt at ease in a house that
could tolerate dust in its corners and allow as much disorder
to the people living in it as there was in its own arrangement
of rooms and crooked passages, dark cupboards and uneven
stairs.

Lunch was ready for her and Colin in the dining-room, a
light, cold lunch that came mostly out of tins. Jean had very
little interest in food and to spend much money, time or
thought upon it came high on her list of sins. But the chopped
ham and salad was served on plates of old Worcester by a
manservant in a white jacket, and when the baby in a per-
ambulator in the garden set up a wail, it was the wife of the
manservant who ran out from the kitchen to see what had
disturbed her.

Not that Jean was by any means happy about being
waited on by other people. If only she had not been rich, she
could have done her own cooking and run out herself to
comfort her baby. But to achieve that desirable state of
affairs, she would have had to dismiss the Brodskys, who
were refugees and elderly, and though not outstandingly
efficient in their work, had always been very kind to her
and Colin.

Colin chattered during lunch as if he had accepted without
question Jean's injunction that he should drop the subject
that he had raised at the garden gate. But when coffee was
brought, he returned to it, saying suddenly, after a short
silence during which he had lit their cigarettes, " Be honest,
Jean—you can't bear it, can you? "

She hesitated, as if she were wondering whether or not to
pretend that she did not know what he was talking about.
Then she shrugged her shoulders.

" I don't know what to say when I've said so often——"

" Don't worry about what you've said before," he said.
" I want you to say what you really feel, for a change. Say
something new. Because, you see, if you were to tell me that
it makes you terribly unhappy to see me just sitting around,

I think I'd . . . well, you know I'd do anything you really wanted me to, don't you? "

She sighed deeply. " But there's no need for you to work if you don't want to, is there? We've been over it all so often and we've agreed——"

" But it's just my not wanting to that you can't bear," he said. " You try to, you try awfully hard. But you don't really believe your own arguments. So let's start from that point now. Tell me what you'd really like me to do, since you can't stand my going on indefinitely being simply an unusually contented man."

She frowned at the little grey heap of ash in the ash-tray.

" *Are* you contented? " she asked.

" Very," he answered.

" In that case, why do you keep coming back to this? What is it that *you* really want? Is it that you half-wish I'd give you a push to make you do something? "

" Perhaps," he said.

" If it were. . . . But that's something you've got to decide for yourself. I can't. I can't possibly."

" Even though you're a much stronger character than I am? " His smile was sardonic. " Don't you think that if you minded less about exerting power over me through your money, and told me simply what you think I ought to do, it might be better for us both? "

" So you aren't so very happy? "

" I am, but you aren't."

They looked at one another frowningly. The expressions on both their faces might have been of a deep distrust. Then, at the same moment, they laughed.

Standing up, Colin let his hand fall on her short, curling hair.

" All right," he said, " we both know I'm just a lazy devil with occasional flickers of conscience. But I love you—I love everything about you, including your blessed money, and I'm very happy—what more can a man say? But d'you know something? I might—I just might drive over to see Joe and Miriam this week."

" To see if they've got a job for Susan? "

" Yes, that—and to see if Joe, who's good at that kind of thing, could make any suggestions as to how I might at least look as if I were constructively employed, so that you'd have to think up fewer excuses for me."

Jean's fingers lightly touched his cheek.

" You have your virtues, even as you are. I endure you better than you think. But if you do go to see them, mind you come back in time for Fanny's party."

She went to the door and out into the garden.

She went to take a look at the baby, now peacefully asleep under a frilly cot-cover. Yet she stayed there only for a moment. Going indoors again, she went upstairs to a small room, furnished with a desk, a chair, a bookcase and a filing cabinet. It was a cold-looking, stark room, meant more for meditation than for work, because, in spite of herself, Jean had not really a great deal of work to do.

To-day some letters needed answering. She began on them, but her mind soon wandered and after a while she discovered that she hardly knew what she was writing. Discussions with Colin on the subject of his idle life always had the same effect on her. The trouble was that she really did not know what her true feelings on the subject were, or what Colin's were either. Not that he was actually idle. He was usually as fully and zestfully occupied as any well-brought-up child. He looked after the garden, went bird-watching, collected various kinds of insects, took excellent photographs and read a great deal. But no one paid him for the way that he spent his time. In fact, at thirty-three, he behaved like a man who had retired.

True, the retirement appeared to be a singularly happy one. Yet he was right when he insisted that Jean was unable to convince herself finally that there was nothing morally wrong in the situation. Vaguely, uncertainly, she attributed it all to the war and his wounds, which had been terrible. During the long months in hospital, she thought, the hospital in which they had first met and she, a young nurse, had had the care of him, his hold on life had been so precarious and so painful that to live at all might have come to seem an end in itself.

She often told herself that she had no real reasons for worry. Colin loved her and he loved their child, of those two things she was certain and that should have been enough. Her doubts, her severe mind told her, were merely conventional.

Once roused, however, they made her restless. Giving up the attempt to write letters, she went downstairs again and out into the garden, slipped through a gap in the hedge and looked in at the window of the Lynams' sitting-room

She saw Fanny lying stretched out on the sofa. Her shoes were on the floor, her grey hair was tumbled over her forehead, Martin the cat was curled up on her stomach. The room was filled with a flickering light from the logs that were now alight on the hearth. It was a very peaceful scene, or it would have been, but for the look on Fanny's face, as she stared at the photograph that she was holding in both hands.

Jean saw that look only for an instant, because as soon as Fanny saw her at the window, she smiled and beckoned her to come in, yet in that glimpse of her that Jean had had there had been something which suggested to her that Fanny had been considering the efficacy of sticking pins into the photograph.

As Jean came into the sitting-room, Fanny sat up and holding out the photograph, said, " Is there something the matter with me, Jean, or *is* there something peculiar about that face? "

Jean looked at it carefully.

She had seen it before and had looked at it carefully enough then, because a newcomer in the rather intimate little community that had developed in the village during the last few years was naturally a matter of interest.

Some hopes and a slight apprehension had been roused by the thought of Laura Greenslade's coming. But now, because of the mood that Jean was in, the apprehension suddenly dominated all other feelings. For some strange reason, she looked at the face in the photograph with dread, with a distinct feeling that it was malign and dangerous. But as she continued to look at it, the feeling faded, and Jean became convinced that it had been communicated to her by Fanny.

Handing the photograph back, Jean replied, " I can't honestly say I see anything peculiar about it. But this awfully posed sort of affair never tells one anything."

" No, it doesn't, does it ? " Fanny said gratefully. " I expect it's just that I'm scared stiff about the whole business. But won't it be awful for us all if we don't like her ? "

" It always seems to me you like almost everybody," Jean said. She noticed that characteristically Fanny had not expected to be given any explanations of her visit, but had plunged straight into the discussion of her own affairs.

" Anyway, I'm putting on quite a show for her," Fanny said.

" So Colin told me." The sound of a car stopping outside made Jean turn her head to the window. " There's Basil," she said.

" Yes, he telephoned he'd be down this afternoon." Getting up, Fanny gave herself a glance in the old mirror. " God, how my hair needs cutting," she said, frowning. " I'll have to get it done before Saturday. I'm making my special lobster things, of course."

She went to meet her husband.

As he came in he put his hands on her shoulders and kissed her, then seeing Jean, held out his hand to her. Basil Lynam was never casual in his behaviour, he never omitted greetings, never failed to rise to his feet at the right moment or to open doors.

He was fifty-three, a slight, grey-haired man of medium height, a reader in genetics at one of the London colleges. Because Fanny insisted on living so deep in the country that he could not possibly travel daily to his work, he spent only week-ends and odd days in his home. Though he was often pitied for this he never complained about it, saying that in fact it helped him to get a lot of work done. He was very much wrapped up in his work and though he was singularly gentle and in some ways perceptive in his dealings with people, his real interest in them seldom seemed to go deep. For friends he appeared satisfied with those that Fanny made for him. His face was narrow and dark, with bright, very youthful eyes, full of a curious innocence.

B

It was typical of him that though he knew Jean far less intimately than Fanny did, he should notice at once that she had something on her mind. But he did not refer to it until after she had gone. Then, sitting by the fire, while Fanny poured out the tea that she had made, he said, "What's Jean's trouble to-day? The usual one?"

Fanny's forehead wrinkled. "Had she a trouble?" she said. "We were talking about Laura. And I was thinking about the Poulter man too. Clare's coming down, by the way. I wonder why she wants so much to meet the man. It isn't at all like her."

"Jean isn't happy," Basil went on.

"Of course not," Fanny said. "She's too much in love with Colin to be happy. He's in love with her too, but that doesn't help. She can never stop worrying about him."

"Is that what you do when you're in love?" Basil asked with one of his bright, innocent glances at his wife.

"Well, that girl's got everything she can possibly want," Fanny said, "a handsome, adoring husband, a baby, money —and yet she can't stop worrying."

"I'd worry too, if I'd got everything I wanted," Basil said musingly. "Any moment could bring such terrible disaster."

"That's what some moments do anyway," Fanny said. "It's in the nature of things. But Jean's just the worrying type. She ought to have married someone like you, who's good at calming people down. And Colin ought to have married someone like me, because we understand each other. And—and Kit, damn it, ought to have married Susan!" She jolted her tea-cup, spilling some tea on the clean tray-cloth that she had brought out in honour of her husband's presence. "I'll never say this to anybody but you, darling, but I know I'm going to *hate* Laura."

"You aren't," Basil said equably. "As I remember her, she was a quite pleasant and normal young woman. Once we've got used to her——"

"Not normal!" Fanny exclaimed. "You said so yourself."

"I did?" Basil said in a tone of astonishment.

"You did. You said there was something peculiar about her."

" Oh, that," Basil said. " Yes, you're perfectly right, as it happens. I do connect her vaguely with something odd. . . . It'll come back to me suddenly, I expect, unless I'm mistaken · about it. It could have been somebody else."

" But what *was* it? " Fanny demanded. " What was the matter with her? What had she done? "

" Done? " Basil said. " I don't think she'd done anything." The flickering light of the flames was reflected in his eyes, and his thin, dark face reddened with the heat as he bent towards the fire to push one of the logs farther back on the hearth.

CHAPTER FOUR

CLARE FORWOOD saw nothing peculiar about Laura Greenslade when she called for her at ten o'clock on the following Saturday morning.

To Clare this was a matter for regret. With the peculiarities of people she felt at home, but normality, or that quality which she thought of as normality, without ever quite believing in its existence, frightened her out of her wits.

Seeing a slim, dark, well-tailored young woman, quietly self-assured in manner, come down the stairs to meet her, Clare felt on the defensive, inferior and vulnerable, and would have liked to turn tail immediately and hurry back to the safety of her Hampstead flat.

She was in a highly nervous state that morning, and was bitterly regretting the impulse that had made her ask Fanny Lynam to arrange a meeting for her with Sir Peter Poulter. At the time of asking her, Clare had not thought seriously that Fanny would really do anything about her request. But Fanny was unpredictable. She made promises easily, and could usually be safely trusted to forget them. Yet now and again she insisted on overcoming all obstacles and carrying out some promise to the last letter. To Clare, who in fact intensely disliked any interference with the solitary routine of her life, whatever she might occasionally say to the contrary, this was a very dangerous characteristic. In anyone but Fanny, whom she had known for over thirty years of her life, she would probably not have tolerated it.

They had met first as students in a dramatic school. That Clare should ever have thought of the stage as a career now seemed wholly fantastic to herself. Probably if her mother had not been an actress and expected it of her, she would never have attempted it. Yet her friends remembered that she had had a certain talent. She had also had one or two difficult love-affairs, resulting in nervous calamity for all concerned. But fortunately she had been rescued from this existence by bad health and a small private income. In increasing solitariness, keeping only a few old friends whom she consented to see at longer and longer intervals, and very seldom making even a new acquaintance, she had developed her greater talent, acquiring, to her own deep astonishment, considerable fame.

In appearance she was rather like an underpaid governess, with an odd, scared gentility about her, though inward-looking, brooding eyes, under untidy grey eyebrows and a heavy brow, gave her face a formidable character of which she was quite unaware. She thought of herself as being merely plain and colourless and it would have surprised her to know that Laura Greenslade, coming down the stairs, had no difficulty at all in identifying the small, shabby woman waiting for her in the hall as the distinguished novelist.

Clare flushed when Laura addressed her, was mono-syllabic and awkwardly excitable. Laura was the type of woman who at a first encounter always roused in her upsetting emotions of contempt and envy. She thought of women like her as models for suburban housewives, figures stepping straight out of the women's magazines, equipped with beauty, poise, and unerring dress-sense and no emotional problems that could not be solved for ever in five thousand words.

Also, for reasons that Clare had arduously but never quite successfully analysed, she expected this type of woman to be antagonistic to herself, so that, at the first pleasant and friendly remark from such a one, she felt, after a shock of disbelief, a glow of gratitude and pleasure. While the second feeling lasted, Clare was liable to discover unusual intelligence, true charm and grace of spirit in the person.

The third stage came when Clare began to notice some comforting human failing in this exquisite creation of her own fantasy, and suddenly forgetting her fears, quickly allowed herself to become bored by her as a human being, though sometimes sharply interested in her as a specimen.

She reached the third stage this morning after about an hour's driving in her small 1935 Morris. She always drove slowly, with erratic over-caution. Laura had appeared to be admirably indifferent to the hazards of it, talking quietly and delightfully about the pleasure that she had taken in reading Clare's books, and except that Laura's face and voice were somewhat expressionless, Clare had been able to perceive no fault in her of any kind. And that expressionlessness, after all, was proper to her type. That oval face with its regular features and creaseless skin was not meant to have its smooth planes disturbed by the lights and shadows of strong feeling. The mouth, small and full-lipped with perfect teeth, the china-blue eyes, the dark hair pulled back from the face with a sleek severity, fashionable at the moment, should not be marred, Clare had thought, by animation. Yet presently, and in spite of an almost obstinate desire in herself not to notice it, Clare had had to recognise that feeling had crept into the face and the voice, also that it was precisely the kind of feeling which most roused her often unscrupulous, almost brutal curiosity. It was feeling, that is to say, which she knew that Laura had not intended to betray.

The chance to learn something about someone else's secrets without their knowing that she was doing so was to Clare like the scent of blood to a bloodhound. Unconsciously, her posture became more relaxed. Her shyness left her.

" Yes," she had just said in reply to Laura's last remark, " I've known Fanny for most of my life. I have a very great affection for her."

" So has Kit," Laura had said. " He's always telling me about what a wonderful person she is. She's warm-hearted and generous and sincere. I'm longing to meet her."

But that, Clare had known at once, had been a lie. Or at

least, it had not been quite, absolutely, undeniably true. Laura was at least a little bit afraid of meeting Fanny. Afraid, that was it.

Secret fears and hatreds were the subject of nearly all Clare's writing. They were the only emotions of which she had any deep understanding.

Laura was going on, " She's been almost like Kit's mother, hasn't she? I wonder why she never had any children of her own."

" Her first marriage wasn't conducive to it," Clare said, " and by the time she married Basil, she was past it."

" I expect she'll miss Kit terribly then when he leaves her," Laura said.

To this at first Clare made no reply. She thought it over, remembering what Fanny had said to her a few days before on the telephone about dividing the house.

At last she said, " Then you're going to live in London, are you? "

" I expect so," Laura said. " I'll have to keep my work going at least until Kit's established himself, and it's the best place for me to be. And it'll be the best place for Kit too, I think."

" What is he planning to do? "

" He wants to get into advertising."

" Now that surprises me," Clare said. " I thought he liked to work with his hands."

" He'll go on with that as a hobby, naturally."

" But you don't think there's much of a living in it? "

" Do you? "

" I suppose not—in this day and age."

" It isn't as if he's outstandingly gifted at it either," Laura said. " He isn't an artist of any kind, he's just a reasonably good carpainter. And I believe he's got a flare in the other direction. That's the side of the antique business that's really interested him, the buying and selling."

" And you think you can get him floated in London, even though he's had so little experience? " Clare said.

" Oh yes, I know lots of people," Laura answered carelessly.

Clare said no more just then. Having recognised the fear

in Laura, she had become capable of recognising other qualities, instead of stopping short at her well-finished appearance. She could recognise now a great strength of will in the girl, maintained by a clear knowledge of what she wanted. Clare herself had an immense fund of determination, but was aware of confusion in the way she directed it. Laura, she realised, had thought clearly and was probably prepared to act ruthlessly. She knew she might have a fight on her hands for the possession of Kit, was a little apprehensive, but had admitted her fear to herself and made up her mind to have victory on her own terms.

Clare felt sorry for Fanny, who never thought clearly about anything. Yet quite likely, Laura's way was the best way for all of them, particularly for Kit. On this point Clare was careful to avoid forming an opinion.

Laura and Fanny met, a little later, with exclamations of delight. Basil also, shaking Laura's hand, expressed great pleasure at meeting her again after so many years.

" Then you remember me, Dr. Lynam? " Laura said with surprise, seeming to be very pleased by this.

" He's just pretending to, my dear," Fanny said cheerfully. " He's got the worst memory in the world."

She had dressed for the occasion with more care than usual, in a dress of large black and white checks, high-heeled red slippers, and a pair of long, gold, antique Spanish ear-rings. Outrageous as this might have been on her heavy, uncorseted body and with her hair as ungroomed as ever, in an odd, raffish way, of which she had never quite lost the secret, it had a kind of smartness.

" Not at all," Basil said primly. " I remember you perfectly."

Kit, looking excited and shy, though determined to show neither feeling, made a great fuss of Clare. He might almost have had no interest in Laura at all. Smiling at it, she exchanged an understanding glance with Fanny. The two of them went upstairs together to the room that had been made ready for Laura.

She exclaimed with admiration of the house as she went.

"It's perfect," Clare heard her say. "It's unbelievable. How I would love to live in a house like this."

"I'll explain some ideas I've had about that afterwards," Fanny answered happily, as Clare went into the sitting-room with Basil, who gave her sherry.

Kit fidgeted in and out of the room, going half-way up the stairs and coming down again, waiting for the first chance to have Laura to himself for a few minutes. Martin the cat, with the perverse instinct by which cats can generally recognise at once the people who dread them, rubbed himself, purring, against Clare's ankles. Basil, who knew her peculiarity about cats, picked Martin up, opened a window and tossed him out into the garden.

"Thank you," she said. "You may have a bad memory, but you never forget anything that concerns other people's comfort."

"I haven't a bad memory," Basil replied. "That's one of Fanny's fictions. I recognised that girl at once, and as I used hardly to know her, I don't think that's at all bad."

"It's a good many years since you saw her, is it?" Clare asked, sipping her sherry.

"Ten, at least," Basil said.

"She's a very good-looking young woman."

"Yes, indeed."

"So she ought to be easy to remember."

"But I see so many good-looking young women in my job. They come in dozens every year."

"Laura is above the average," Clare said. "And didn't Fanny tell me something about some peculiarity of hers that you'd remembered?"

"That I *hadn't* remembered." His bright, dark eyes had mischief in them. "That was the whole point of it."

"Now, Basil," Clare said, smiling a little in response, "what's all this?"

"I really didn't remember it at first," he said, "and afterwards . . . Well, it's too complicated to explain and not really at all interesting."

"But surely——"

"No, no," he said, "really it isn't."

" But you want Fanny to go on thinking that Laura has dark secrets in her past? "

" She *has* dark secrets," Basil said. " You've only to take a look at her to be sure of it. And Fanny will find out all about them long before I do."

" But oughtn't you to explain whatever this other thing is to Fanny? "

" There are some things you can't explain to Fanny, because they don't interest her. But now tell me, Clare, why are you lying in wait for Sir Peter Poulter? "

Clare drank some more sherry, looked at the crackling logs in the big fireplace, moved her feet about, then trying to sound flippant said, " That's *my* dark secret."

" Have you met him before? "

" Oh no. And if I'd thought that Fanny would really . . . well, you know, I was just talking and . . . What sort of person is he, Basil? "

" I haven't met him either," Basil said, " He's lived very much as a recluse since he took Dene House. He's supposed to be a very sick man—heart, I think. That's probably why he settled in an out-of-the-way place like this. Now and again his house fills up with visitors, but mostly he seems to be alone with two old servants."

" Strange for a man like that—after the sort of life he must have lived," Clare said. " But he lived in these parts when he was a boy. Did you know that? "

" No," Basil said. " Are you sure? I've never heard it said anywhere here."

" Yes," Clare said. " I'm sure."

" So his coming here could be a sort of coming home to die," Basil suggested.

The door opened and Fanny came in, followed by Laura and Kit.

" Who's going to die? " Fanny asked cheerfully.

" We were talking about Sir Peter Poulter," Basil said.

" Petie? " Laura exclaimed excitedly. " Don't tell me you know him."

Fanny shot a quick look at her, then crossed to the table where the drinks were.

" He's coming to cocktails this evening," she said casually.
" Sherry, Laura? "

" Thank you. Well, how marvellous. He gave me my
first job," Laura said with enthusiasm. " I simply love him.
He's as tough as nails, of course, and utterly ruthless, but
very sweet if he happened to like you, and—well, he did like
me."

She gave a little laugh and gave Kit a sidelong look. " Of
course he was old enough to be my grandfather."

" But who says he's going to die, even if he is somebody's
grandfather? " Fanny asked. There were times when it was
difficult to keep her mind on the same subject for more than
a moment and other times when it utterly refused to be
dislodged. There was anxiety in her tone now, almost as if
she feared Sir Peter's death might happen at her cocktail
party.

" He's nobody's grandfather," Clare said. " His sons were
both killed in the war."

This remark brought an uneasy seriousness into the room.
Clare had spoken with the curious emphasis which had
entered her voice each time she had spoken of Sir Peter. But
as if she saw that her words had been in the wrong key, she
went on quickly, " Has Fanny been showing you the house,
Laura? "

There was a pause before Laura answered, " Yes. It's
perfectly lovely."

But that was in the wrong key too, subdued and somehow
not convincing. Clare saw Kit, whose blue eyes had
settled on Laura's face in a long, dreaming stare, wrinkle his
forehead slightly, as if he were not quite sure that he had
heard her correctly.

" Yes, and I've been showing her how we could divide it
up," Fanny said. " As it used to be two cottages, it'd be
quite easy. It's just a case of putting a wall back and doing
some plumbing. It'll be rather fun to work it out."

" But it'll spoil your lovely house," Laura said. " I'd hate
to think of doing that."

" It won't spoil it at all," Fanny said.

" Oh, but——"

" Not at all," Fanny said firmly. " As I told you, it's how it was meant to be. Now let's go and have lunch."

She steered them all through to the dining-room.

She was in a nervous mood, which showed by the way that her florid face had reddened as soon as she had drunk a little sherry and also by the way, as they all sat down, that she kept on talking. But it was a gay kind of nervousness and she seemed to be pleased with Laura. She asked her a great many questions about her journalistic work and also about her child. Because of the child, Fanny said, perhaps the young couple should take over the larger part of the house, the better part. Again Laura protested, saying that she could never allow Fanny and Basil to put themselves out in such a way.

Clare was interested in Laura's reaction to Fanny. It seemed to Clare that Laura found herself liking Fanny far more than she had expected and that this set her some kind of problem for which she had been unprepared. There was a wariness about her, a look of waiting. Her face, her large blue eyes, her small, pretty mouth, were as unexpressive as ever, but there was tension in the poise of her small, sleek, dark head and in the movements of her hands.

She had adopted a slightly childish manner towards Fanny, deprecating and 'excessively modest, as if she were a very young and inexperienced girl, rather than a widow of thirty-two or three, mother of a child and a tolerable success in her profession. If Fanny thought that there was anything inappropriate about this, she did not show it, but talked on cheerfully. Basil was his usual quiet self, attentive and apparently charmed, but Kit, almost unable to remove his eyes from Laura's face, had a bewildered air, a look of raised eyebrows, of being ready to make a protest of some sort.

A ludicrous memory came to Clare. She had once gone to a market and bought a chicken to cook for a small dinner-party that she had been giving that same evening. The stall-holder had taken the chicken behind the counter and wrapped it up in paper. When Clare had reached home, she had removed the wrappings and found inside not a chicken but two widgeons. As it turned out, they had been excellent and

the dinner quite successful. Nevertheless the incident had
been disconcerting. She had not quite succeeded, somehow,
in adjusting herself to the widgeons. And that was how Kit
looked now, just as if he had bought himself a chicken in the
market and it had turned into two small, plump widgeons.

When lunch was over, Fanny sent Laura and Kit away and
took Clare into the kitchen to help her with the washing-up.

The kitchen, entirely modernised, with plenty of stainless
steel and built-in cupboards, was littered with Fanny's pre-
parations for the party. She was a very untidy cook and
when she came out from the dining-room, carrying a pile of
plates, there was hardly any space where she could put them
down.

Making some room by thrusting at a heap of saucepans
with an elbow, she sank into a chair, saying with a sigh,
" Let's have a quiet cigarette before we get started."

It irked Clare to sit in the untidy kitchen, but she perched
on the edge of a chair and accepted one of Fanny's cigarettes.

" What," she said, pointing at a plate on the table in front
of her, " are these things? "

" Lobster patties," Fanny said.

" The *specialité de la maison?* "

" That's right. They're an awful job to make, but they
really are awfully good. Of course I don't make the pastry
cases. Mine always come as heavy as lead and topple over
sideways. I get them made by Mrs. Webb in the village."

" What d'you put into them? " Clare asked interestedly.

" Oh, brandy and wine and garlic and so on—and lobster,
of course. Try one."

" Not just after ice-cream. But they certainly look
delicious."

Fanny gave a great yawn and rubbed the back of her wrist
against her forehead.

" I couldn't sleep last night," she said.

" Too worried? " Clare asked.

" No, I'm not worried—why should I be? " Fanny said.
" Just excited. It's quite an event, after all, Kit getting
married."

" And what do you think about the girl? "

Quickly Fanny answered, " Charming. She *is* charming, don't you think Clare? "

" Unquestionably," Clare said.

" The only trouble is," Fanny said, " she doesn't seem to me like the sort of girl who'll fit in down here and Kit simply won't go anywhere else. I've often tried to get him to see that it isn't good for him, being as dependent on me as he is, but short of telling him I'm shutting down the shop, I don't think he'll ever pay any attention to me. Of course I've only kept the antique business going on his account. I started it to have something to do here, and then when Kit came out of the army and hadn't a job and didn't seem to know what to do with himself, I thought perhaps he could help me with the buying and learn something about repairing furniture and so on. I only meant it to last until he found something better. But then he got so keen on it he won't even look for anything else. And I know it isn't good for him, holding on to me like that, and it doesn't actually pay Basil and me at all to keep the shop going—I just about get Kit's salary out of it—and now with his marrying and all . . ." She paused, looking questioningly at Clare, as if she expected her to supply an answer to something that she had not been asked.

Clare said nothing. Then she got up briskly and moved to the sink.

" Let's get all this stuff out of the way," she said. " It gets on my nerves."

With great speed she started sorting out plates, bowls and pans into neat piles.

Fanny chuckled. Then she got up lethargically, keeping her cigarette at the corner of her mouth, reached for a cloth from a line over her head and stood waiting for some dishes to dry.

After a minute or two she went on, " Kit *ought* to go away from me. I know it. His marrying a girl like Laura shows it. He's picked someone as unlike me as he can find and that must mean that really he wants to get away from me."

" I wonder," Clare said, " if, in his view, she is so very unlike you."

" Good heavens, Clare! "

" I said, in *his* view."

" Then he must have a good memory," Fanny said sardonically. She was ruminatively polishing a glass that Clare had just put down on the draining-board. " Well, I suppose it'll work itself out somehow. Meanwhile, I think I'll get George Chagwell in to take a look at the house and make a rough estimate for the alterations. He's just a country builder, but he's awfully reliable and he does understand these old houses."

Basil, coming into the kitchen just then, overheard her last two sentences.

" I don't think you need bother with Chagwell," he said.

His voice was troubled. The sound of it made Clare look round at him from her work at the sink. He was standing by the table, gazing down absently at the lobster patties.

But Fanny appeared not to have noticed anything unusual in his way of speaking.

" Would you put those things on the big Mason dish, Basil, and pop them into the larder? " she said. " Then we can get this table really cleared."

He went to a cupboard and started looking amongst disorderly heaps of crockery for the dish she wanted.

" What's the trouble, Basil? " Clare asked. " What's happened? "

" Nothing much at present, to the best of my knowledge," he replied. " But I don't think we shall have to divide our house."

" But . . ." Fanny let her hands fall to her sides and stood still, staring at him.

" I couldn't help overhearing a part of what sounded like a very violent argument," he said. " I didn't hear what Kit said, but Laura's voice was raised in what sounded like the greatest excitement. She was telling Kit that she had no intention at all of living down here and that wherever they go she had in any case no intention of sharing a house with anybody. I have to admit . . ." He withdrew his head from the cupboard, emerging with a large oval dish in his hands. Putting it on the table, he started arranging the lobster patties on it with great care. " I have to admit that I have a certain sympathy with her. I shouldn't have liked to settle too close to any member of my own family when I first got married. We're none of us suitably educated any more for a tribal way of living."

"Tribal!" Fanny muttered. She said nothing else, and after a moment went on drying the silver that Clare was clattering on to the draining-board. But her face, in spite of what she had said to Clare about her wish that Kit would become independent of her, had become empty and colourless. She seemed to be having difficulty with her breathing, almost as if she were fighting to hold back tears.

Just then, from the garden, a voice called her, "Fanny!"

It was Jean Gregory. She came hurrying into the kitchen by the back door, carrying a great armful of almond blossom. Above the cloud of pink flowers, clinging to the angular, leafless twigs, her face was unusually flushed.

"I brought you these in case you'd like them to decorate the room for your party," she said, "because—because Colin and I can't come." Her flush mounted as she said it.

"You and Colin can't come?" Fanny said incredulously. "But you said——"

"Yes, but a horrible—a perfectly horrible—thing has happened." Jean held the flowers out in front of her stiffly, as if she felt they provided her with a shield. "Colin and Tom Mordue have had the most frightful quarrel and after the things Tom said to Colin, I won't—I simply won't—let him stay in the same room with him. So if Tom's coming— I'm awfully sorry, Fanny, and I'm terrified that perhaps you won't forgive me—but if Tom's coming, Colin and I can't!"

CHAPTER FIVE

FANNY SAT DOWN. With one hand she clawed at her hair, with the other she groped blindly for a cigarette. Basil put one into her mouth and lit it for her.

"I'm awfully sorry, Fanny, awfully," Jean went on

quickly. She looked down at the flowers now as if she were wondering why she had brought them.

" It can't be helped," Fanny said wearily. " What happened? "

" It's a complicated story." Jean turned to Basil. " Are these any use? If they aren't——"

" They're beautiful," he said, taking the armful of blossom. " We've no almond in our garden. I always look at yours with envy."

" What happened? " Fanny repeated.

" It was about Susan," Jean said. " Colin got an idea that something ought to be done about Susan now that—now that——"

" Say it," Fanny said. " Now that Kit's thrown her over— damn him! "

Jean looked startled. " Damn him? Why? "

" Never mind," Fanny said. " But we all know that's what's happened."

" Well, it was because of that," Jean said. " Colin got it into his head that it would be a good thing for Susan to go away. He thought if she stayed here she'd get into the habit of being pitied by everyone and that that would be very bad for her. So two days ago he went to see some friends of ours who live in Essex. They've got four children and they always seem to be in need of someone to help with them. So Colin drove over——"

" Wait a minute," Fanny said. " *Colin* thought of all this all by himself? "

" Yes, certainly," Jean said.

" It wasn't really you? "

Jean gave an emphatic shake of her head.

Fanny made a helpless gesture. " I shall never get to under- stand anything about people—never," she said. " Go on."

" Well, Colin drove over to see Joe and Miriam," Jean said, " and as it happened, their most recent nurse had just got married, so they were delighted to hear about Susan and said that whatever pay she was getting at the minute, they'd give her more. So Colin came home very pleased with him- self and yesterday evening we got hold of Susan and put the idea to her—cautiously, of course. She was cautious too and said she'd have to think it over, but I believe she was really awfully pleased. She seemed to get more and more interested in the scheme as the evening went on, though she kept saying that she couldn't possibly go at once, because that wouldn't be fair on the people she's with now, who've been very good to her. And right at the end she said she'd have to talk it over with her parents. Till then I thought she was going to make up her mind for herself, but just when she was leaving she said it would depend a lot on what Tom and Minnie thought. And that's what made the trouble."

Basil was arranging the flowers in a tall stoneware jug. "Tom was angry?" he asked with that air of quiet concern which was his response to most of the more unpleasant things of life.

Jean gave a whistle. "Honestly," she said, "I've never seen anything like it. I've seen him make some horrible scenes, but never one that came near this one. If he'd settled down with a paper and pencil to make a list of all the worst insults he could offer Colin and me——"

"You too?" Basil said gravely, as if insulting Colin were only a venial offence, but insulting Jean a serious matter. "Dear, dear."

"Well, not directly," Jean said. "But he insulted me through Colin. And as I was saying, if he'd taken hours thinking out all the most outrageous things he could say——"

"He probably did," Fanny said.

"I really shouldn't be surprised," Jean agreed. "It was the most extraordinary exhibition I've ever seen. He came in just before lunch. At first I thought he was drunk, his face was so red and his manner was so wild, but actually I don't think he'd had a single drink. And he—he called Colin . . ." The painful flush returned to her pale cheeks. She hesitated, then went on, "Well, it doesn't matter what he actually said. It was all about Colin's interfering in Susan's private affairs because he—he hadn't enough to occupy himself. Only he put it in such a horrible way."

Fanny and Basil exchanged a glance.

"And what did Colin do?" Fanny asked.

" Nothing at all," Jean said excitedly. " Absolutely
nothing. You know what he's like. He never loses his temper.
He never bothers to defend himself if people attack him. He
just sat there looking conciliatory and saying that he quite
understood Tom's feelings—until *I* lost my temper. I wasn't
going to let anyone say those things to my husband. So I
started telling him a few of the things I've thought about
him for a long time. So then Tom ordered me to keep out
of it, just as if he was still a schoolmaster and I was one of
his miserable pupils, and then Colin . . ." Her voice trembled
and stopped.

" Colin got wild too? " Fanny suggested.

" No," Jean said. " At least—well, I'm not sure. I'm not
sure what it meant. . . ."

" Something he said? "

" No, the way he started to laugh. He just roared with
laughter until Tom rushed out of the house."

" Then at least it coped with the situation," Fanny said.

" Yes, but . . ." Jean stopped again. Her voice was still
unsteady. " I didn't like it. I got scared suddenly. And that's
why . . . I didn't mean to say this, but once I started it just
went on coming. Fanny, I don't think those two ought to
meet again to-day."

Fanny gave a reluctant nod. " My poor party," she said.
" But I know how you feel—though they'll probably make it
up quite soon over a pint in The Waggoners."

With a look of doubt in her eyes, Jean said, " Probably—
I hope so. Colin says even now that he isn't angry, and that
he could have told me beforehand that it was going to happen
exactly like that. He said he was quite prepared for it and
really did understand Tom's feelings, because Tom naturally
took the whole thing as a deliberate criticism of him and his
care for his daughter. And actually Colin said he didn't at all
mind meeting Tom this evening and wanted to come to the
party. So then I took a high line and said I'd been insulted
unforgivably by Tom and I utterly refused to be in the
same room with him again, so there wasn't much Colin could
do but agree that we shouldn't come. Fanny, I'm sorry, I'm
terribly sorry about it, but I think it would be much more

likely to upset your party if we did come than if we didn't."

"It can't be helped," Fanny said, "though I wish it was you and Colin who were coming and Tom who'd decided to stay away. But things never work out like that. Lunatics like Tom never withdraw from anything." She gave a mournful smile at Jean. "Don't worry, my dear. They'll patch it up in a day or two. We'll see you both soon?"

"Oh yes—yes, of course," Jean said gratefully. She paused for a moment as if there was something more she intended to say, but then abruptly left them, her wide grey coat swirling about her as she turned.

Fanny let out a long breath, then looked at Clare, who had been standing unobtrusively by the sink, quietly continuing with the washing-up.

"Having fun?" Fanny asked.

"I'd have had more fun if I'd understood the terrible insults that Mr. Mordue hurled at Mr. Gregory," Clare replied. "According to my understanding of the story, he merely called him a busybody, which unquestionably Mr. Gregory was."

"That's because you don't know the set-up," Fanny said. "It's quite obvious what really happened. Tom turned on Colin and abused him for living on his wife's money— I wouldn't put it past Tom, when he's in one of those moods, to have called Colin a gigolo—and any criticism of Colin on those lines is the one thing on earth that Jean won't tolerate."

"Naturally—whether it's true or not," Clare said. "Is it true?"

"It's just silliness." Fanny looked round the kitchen vaguely, seeming rather surprised at the tidiness that had gradually been achieved there. "I think I'll go and lie down for a bit," she said. "You two can talk to each other."

She went out, leaving Clare and Basil a free hand in the kitchen.

Going upstairs to the bedroom she shared with Basil, she threw herself down on the patchwork bedspread that covered the bed. Her cheerfulness at lunch had changed into a mood of appalling depression. Fanny hated all conflict and generally found ways of avoiding it, but when she failed in this, she at

once became despairingly convinced that the particular conflict would never end.   There again, she thought, she and
Colin were alike.   She could easily imagine herself, in circumstances where a quarrel was being forced upon her,
taking refuge, as Colin had, in the laughter that had so dis-
mayed Jean.   It had been semi-hysterical laughter, of course,
which was why Jean had been frightened by it.

For some minutes Fanny lay quite still, then she fumbled
for the usual cigarette and started to puff smoke at the low
ceiling.   The sense of extreme depression lasted only for a
little while, then her resilient nature helped her to see the
brighter side of things.   If her various friends wanted to
quarrel with one another, at least none of them seemed to
want to quarrel with her.   If Laura was not the sister-in-law
that she would have chosen, at least she seemed to want to
be liked.   If poor Susan, of whom Fanny was genuinely fond,
had a broken heart, at least she was young enough and enter-
prising enough to set about getting it mended.   And if other
people were sometimes a trial to one's patience, at least Basil,
at any time of crisis, never failed one.

As always, when darkness covered Fanny's earth, her
troubled mind groped towards thoughts of Basil and found
them deeply comforting.

She had slipped into a light doze, her cigarette consuming
itself in the ash-tray on the table by the bed, when a step in
the passage and a light tap on her door disturbed her.   She
called out a sleepy answer, the door opened and Kit came
in.

She saw at once that there was something unusual about
the look on his face, though at first she could not interpret it.
Afterwards she thought that more than anything else it had
been a look of tension, of waiting, as if he felt sure that some
extraordinary thing were about to happen and was trying
to force himself to bear the strain of suspense without pro-
testing at it.

" Have you got any aspirin? " he asked in a quiet, flat
voice.

" Probably," Fanny said.   " Why, have you got a head? "

" Laura has," he answered, coming into the room and

walking over to Fanny's dressing-table. He pulled open a drawer. " Where is it—in here? "

" I expect so."

He fumbled about amongst handkerchiefs and scarves.

" She gets awful heads," he said. " They lay her out completely for hours." His tone was still dull and empty, as if he were carefully avoiding talking about what was in his mind.

" Hours? " Fanny said in sharp alarm. " You don't mean she's going to be laid out flat for hours *now*? "

" Quite likely." His voice suddenly rose in nervous exasperation. " Where are the bloody things? I can't find them! "

Fanny got heavily to her feet and went over to the dressing-table.

" There they are, right in front of you," she said, picking up the bottle of aspirins that Kit's hand had been almost touching. " The way you never can find anything for yourself. . . . Has she really got a bad headache, Kit? "

" It's bad enough that she's gone to lie down," he said.

" And she may have to lie down for hours? "

" I said that's quite likely, didn't I? "

" And not come to my party? "

" I don't expect she'll feel much like drinks if her head's splitting."

Fanny sat down at the dressing-table. She stared at her face in the glass. She stared at it with a look of deepening disfavour, as if in some way it had just let her down unforgiveably.

" You've been quarrelling, haven't you? " she said. " Is that why she's got a headache? "

" She's gone in for them all her life," Kit answered, his voice toneless once more. " They can happen at any time. It's just bad luck that one's happening to-day."

" You don't think it's just that she doesn't want to come to the party? "

" Why shouldn't she want to come? "

" Perhaps because Susan's coming."

" Why should she mind that? "

Fanny picked up her comb and wrenched it through her short, rough hair.

" Doesn't she know about Susan? " she asked.

" For God's sake, what is there to know? " Kit demanded in a thin, tense voice.

" I wish I really knew," Fanny muttered. " Anyway, everything seems to be a mess—my poor party particularly."

" And I wish you'd stop dropping hints about Susan," Kit said, going towards the door, the bottle of aspirins held in a clenched hand as if it were a bomb that he was preparing to throw. " There never was anything on Susan's side, except that she quite liked me. D'you think I'd have let you invite her to-day or that she'd have agreed to come, if there'd been more than that? "

" I don't know," Fanny said. " I don't know what people are capable of. Sometimes I feel I don't know anything about them."

" You might be right at that," Kit said and walked out.

Fanny went on pulling the comb through her hair. She went on looking at herself. She went on searching for something in her own reflection that at the moment she could not find there. Then she dabbed clumsily at her face with a powder-puff, reached for a bottle of perfume, put rather too much of it on her neck and her wrists, got to her feet with a sigh and went downstairs.

She found Basil alone in the sitting-room. He was reading some sort of scientific text-book while Martin the cat purred on his stomach and Spike the dog dozed before the fire. The room had been made ready for the party. Glasses and bottles were set out on a table. Saucers of salted almonds, olives and such things had been placed in strategic positions. Jean's armful of almond blossom filled the window.

Basil glanced up from his book and said at once, " From the look of you, you could do with a drink before people start coming."

Fanny dropped into a chair, saying, " Bless you, my darling. What in this world would I do without you? "

Without consulting her, he brought her a whisky and soda. She took a gulp of it, coughed and said hoarsely, " Not that anyone's likely to come. Laura's got a bad headache and has gone to lie down. I don't know if that's because of the quarrel you said she was having with Kit, or because of Susan, but whichever it is, she's keeping out of the way. And Kit's in a stinking temper."

" With her? "

" With me. I said too much as usual."

" Well, if only the Mordues would think up some good reason for not coming," Basil said, " we'd have a nice quiet evening."

" Where's Clare? " Fanny asked.

" Changing her dress. Which reminds me, I'd better go and change too."

" You look all right to me." To Fanny he always looked as if his shirt had just been laundered, his suit just pressed, his shoes just polished. This result he mysteriously achieved without any effort that was apparent to her and without any help from her. But he had his firm code, also mysterious to her, of what he must wear at what time and it was useless for her to try to interfere with it. He made no reply to her now, but, suddenly in a hurry, went out.

Fanny swallowed some more of her drink and found herself beginning to feel better. Another few gulps, she thought, and she would probably be feeling quite human. The room looked charming and felt very peaceful. If only, as Basil had suggested, nobody at all would come and he, she, and Clare could have a nice quiet evening together with all those bottles and the good things to eat, it would really be the best possible thing that could happen.

The bell rang.

Fanny started to her feet. She had not heard the creak of the garden gate that usually warned her of visitors, or the sound of any footsteps on the path, so that the shrill sound of the bell had caught her by surprise. She swallowed the rest of her drink hurriedly, put the used glass down in an inconspicuous place, and went to open the door.

An elderly man, tall, stooping and white-haired, stood in the doorway.

" I'm afraid I'm rather early," he said, smiling hesitantly.

The smile did Fanny a world of good. In an instant she was delighted that there was going to be a party, that guests were arriving.

" You couldn't be too early, Sir Peter," she said, holding out her hand.

Sir Peter Poulter took it in his, then lowering his head to avoid knocking it in the low doorway, he stepped inside.

At that moment Clare appeared from the kitchen, holding out before her the dish of lobster patties.

CHAPTER SIX

FANNY INTRODUCED them to each other as they stood in the narrow, stone-flagged passage. She was used to Clare's odd behaviour on meeting strangers and when Clare fixed a peculiarly intent and curious stare on Sir Peter's face and said not a word in answer to his greeting, but went on holding out the dish in front of her, as if she expected him to help himself then and there, Fanny was not much put out. She had done what Clare had asked, arranging a meeting for her with Sir Peter. What Clare chose to do about it now was her own affair.

Fanny led them into the sitting-room.

Whatever Clare's motives for desiring the meeting might be, it was apparent that she had dressed for it with greater care than usual. She was wearing her black velvet. This was a garment that she had owned for at least ten years and that she brought out only on very special occasions. It had a full skirt that reached almost to her ankles and a queer little short jacket with old garnet buttons on it. Some precious lace, held by a garnet brooch, fell over the collar of the jacket. For once Clare was wearing high heels and a little powder and lipstick, while a very beautiful little bead bag dangled on a thin gold chain from her arm. The result she had achieved somehow emphasised her usual look of being an underpaid, exceedingly genteel governess, a governess who just now was painstakingly dressed up in her best. At the same time it had that quality of unconscious distinction that never deserted her.

Sir Peter expressed his pleasure at meeting a writer whose work he so much admired, at which Clare looked startled and embarrassed, as if she did not really believe that he could ever have heard of her. But as Fanny poured out drinks for them, he went on to speak of certain characters in her books with genuine acquaintance. Clare at first responded with a look of pain and confusion, but by degrees allowed herself to enjoy the pleasure of accepting his praise and beamed and almost trembled with happiness.

There was a quiet directness about his way of speaking, a simplicity and informality that expressed very pleasantly a great self-assurance. He was a strikingly handsome old man, though his face was deeply lined, while his heavy brow had the waxen look of extreme age or of serious illness and his eyes, shadowed by shaggy white eyebrows, were restless. The big hand, on which the skin looked dry and lifeless, holding the glass that Fanny had brought to him, was not quite steady.

The next guest to arrive was Mrs. McLean, the doctor's wife. Her husband, she explained, had been called out to attend to a boy who had fallen off a bicycle, but if he was through with the boy in time, would look in later. She was a pleasant, talkative woman, whom it was strange to see, Fanny thought, without gardening gloves and a pair of sécateurs in her hand. Fastening on Basil, who had come downstairs just before she arrived, she plunged into a discussion with him of the best position in her garden for a certain lilac bush. She was always seeking counsel about this bush, which had already been moved a number of times, but which had never yet prospered as in her view it should have done.

Soon she was asking Sir Peter his opinion about it. To Fanny's surprise, he appeared to be as interested in lilac bushes as in Clare Forwood's books, and seemed sufficiently knowledgeable about them to earn Mrs. McLean's high approval.

It was the same presently with Kit, who came in rather

late and with a show of reluctance at appearing at all.
Laura's headache, he said, was still very bad and she could
not possibly come down yet.   Sir Peter spoke to him about
Laura, showing that he remembered having met her and
appearing to take an interest in her and her future.

He even succeeded with Tom Mordue.   The Mordues
arrived so late that Fanny, half-relieved, had almost given
them up and when Tom walked into the room ahead of his
wife and daughter, he had the expression on his face that
meant he was likely to make trouble.   Yet after a drink or
two and a short conversation with Sir Peter, he started to
look quite satisfied with himself, his world and his company.

Afterwards Fanny wondered if the semi-miracle of Tom's
good behaviour might not have been worked by Minnie and
Susan as much as by Sir Peter.   Minnie kept a nervous eye
on him all the evening, as if to remind him of a promise he
had given, and Susan once or twice interrupted a remark of
his that was spoken on a rising note.   Nevertheless, if the two
women had succeeded beforehand in establishing some sort
of control over Tom, it was Sir Peter who put him into a
genuine good humour.

Even Sir Peter's exclamation of pleasure when he had
bitten into one of her lobster patties seemed to Fanny most
perfectly satisfactory.   It had the same sincerity and the same
understanding as he had put into his conversation with
Clare about her books.   Immediately helping himself to a
second, he pressed Fanny not to remove the dish too far out
of his reach.

" I've a latent greed in me," he said, " and I can tell that
these are going to make it hard to control."

" That's the way straight to my heart," Fanny said. "I'm
the sort of cook who needs all the praise she can get."

She passed on with the dish to Susan.

It was Susan who gave her her first pang of doubt about
the lobster patties.   Biting into one, Susan seemed to go rigid
all over before she could swallow.   A look of shock appeared
in her eyes.

Fanny gave her a worried look.

" Is something wrong, Susan? "

"No—oh no, they're delicious," Susan said.

Fanny at that stage still had no doubt of that, so she said, "But I meant, is something wrong with you? You feel all right?"

"Oh yes, absolutely," Susan said. "I think a crumb went down the wrong way."

She had relaxed and the emptiness had gone from her eyes, but she was studying the remains of the lobster patty in her hand with a look of startled disbelief.

Susan was small, light and quick-moving and looked even younger than she was. Her hair was thick and fair, cut in a fringe across her forehead and falling straight to her shoulders. Her face was square, with a short nose and a wide, cheerful mouth. In spite of her smallness, there was something sturdy about her, and in spite of her look of candid simplicity, something self-contained. Fanny had recognised more than once that you could not always tell just where you were with Susan.

For instance, this evening she appeared perfectly serene. She was perhaps a little thoughtful, but when she and Kit settled down in a corner of the room to talk to one another, there was no sign of nervousness about her, no trace of uneasiness. Kit himself seemed to become less tense and nervous while he talked to her.

Wondering if after all everyone had been wrong about Susan, Fanny put the dish she was still holding down on a table and helped herself to a lobster patty.

The next moment she gave a cry.

Everyone looked at her.

She gazed round dazedly, her hand to her throat.

"Good heavens, why did none of you tell me?" she asked, spluttering.

She saw then that the remnants of lobster patties had been inconspicuously jettisoned on the edges of plates. She threw her own into the fire.

"What on earth can I have put into the things?" she asked in horrified bewilderment. "Oh, I'm sorry! Aren't they perfectly unspeakable? Oh, I wish you'd told me straight away instead of pretending they were all right."

"Never mind, dear," Mrs. McLean said, "we all make mistakes and we can sympathise. I served pancakes with lemon at lunch once, and I put salt on them instead of sugar."

"But these tasted quite all right when I'd just made them," Fanny said. "I tried them and they were just how I wanted them. Oh, what can I have done to them?"

Sir Peter crossed the room, stood looking down for a moment at the dish of patties, then helped himself to another. He bit into it, munched it critically, smiled and said, "Perfectly delicious."

"But isn't yours revoltingly bitter?" Fanny asked. "Bitter almost beyond belief?"

"Not at all," he said.

"Mine was," she said. "And so was Susan's. I saw the face she made when she tried to eat it—and I don't wonder!"

"I think you must be excessively critical, Mrs. Lynam," Sir Peter said and helped himself to yet another patty. "I find them absolutely first-rate."

Fanny watched him incredulously as he ate with obvious enjoyment.

"Mine was so bitter it made my tongue curl," she said.

"Mine's just perfect," he answered.

"Perhaps I didn't spoil them all," she said. "I wonder what I could have done to them. Perhaps I spilt something over some of them, detergent or disinfectant or something. Only I don't remember doing anything like that."

"Well, never mind now," Basil said, coming over to the table. "Let's put the rest out of harm's way, before Sir Peter gets one of the bad ones and loses his good impression of the others."

But before he could pick up the dish, Sir Peter said, "Not if I know it! I want these within easy reach—and if no one else will eat them after Mrs. Lynam's terrible condemnation, that's my good fortune. I told you I was greedy."

He carried the dish to a small table close to where he had been standing talking to Clare and resumed his conversation with her.

In a low voice, Fanny said to Susan, " I believe he *does* like them."

" It looks like it," Susan agreed.

" Then some of them must be all right. If he'd eaten one that tasted like mine did, he simply couldn't be putting on a show like that—not even if his upper lip was ever so stiff. Yours *was* frightful too, wasn't it, Susan? "

" Well, it was rather."

" Bitter? "

" Yes."

" What can I have done? What could make them taste like that? God, I feel awful, doing a thing like that. And nobody telling me! "

Susan laughed. " You're among friends, so you shouldn't worry. We all know how good they can be when they go right."

" Thank heaven for Laura's headache, anyway," Fanny said, drawing a deep breath. " What would she have thought of me? Somehow I know that she'd have got just the ones that had been spoilt worst of all." Looking at Sir Peter, she wondered momentarily what he and Clare were talking about so earnestly and whether or not Clare had divulged to him that she had wanted a meeting with him arranged. " He couldn't be pretending, could he, Susan? " she said, still very worried. " I'd feel awful beyond words if I thought he was doing it just to be kind to me. But honestly I don't think he'd be physically capable of it if he'd got one like mine."

" No, as a matter of fact, I don't think so either," Susan said. " I'd really stop worrying."

" But he's so nice, he just might. . . . No, I really don't think he could. Most of them must be all right, and just the ones along one edge or something have had something or other spilt over them." Fanny lit herself a cigarette and drew in a lungful of smoke, breathing it out again slowly and trying to convince herself as she did so that she was quite reassured. " What about the new job that's in the wind, Susan? " she said. " Are you going to take it? "

Susan twisted her glass around in her fingers before she

answered. She watched with concentration the way the
liquid in the glass tilted first to one side, then to the other.
Her square young face had its inscrutable look.

"What would you do if you were me?" she asked at length.

"Take it, I think," Fanny said.

"That's what I thought—until this evening," Susan said.

"What happened this evening?"

"I don't know, that's just the point," Susan said, so quietly
that it might not have been intended for Fanny's ears. She
went on, "It was awfully good of the Gregorys to bother
and I like the sound of the job very much and I know that
sooner or later I ought to get away from home. But I'm not
quite sure that this is actually the right time. . . ."

It looked as if, after a hesitation, she was intending to say
more, but just then her father came up to them.

"Fanny, I owe you an apology," he said.

He said it ironically, as if the suggestion that any action
of his might make apology seriously necessary was naturally
absurd.

Fanny took it in this spirit, saying, "I can't believe my
ears, Tom."

He grinned and patted her shoulders. "You're a nice
girl, Fanny. I'd sooner practise apologising on you than on
anyone I know. But the fact is, I'm sorry, I'm really sorry I
upset Jean and Colin. This girl here and Minnie gave me a
terrible talking to when I got home. I meant it all for the
best, of course, and when I told Colin that if he had any
normal self-respect he'd have something better to do with
his time than spend it sticking his nose into other people's
business, I didn't say anything that I don't mean and wouldn't
be ready to repeat when the occasion warranted it. But I do
see that I ought not to have spoken in that way in front of
Jean. She's a good girl—she's generous and she's loyal and
I have a very high opinion of her. It was just like her to turn
on me as she did, when that good-for-nothing she's married
to couldn't do anything but pretend to be amused at the
home-truths I'd handed out to him."

"But, Tom, I always thought you liked Colin Gregory
quite a lot?" Fanny said.

Tom's small, red, wrinkled face took on an expression of contempt.

"I put up with him," he said. "I put up with him good-humouredly, as I try to with all the other half-educated baboons in this dump——"

"Daddy!" Susan said warningly.

He paused, frowned, then his lipless mouth closed over his large false teeth. He nodded his large head at her, giving his high-pitched, nervous laugh.

"Quite right, girl, quite right," he said. "I was apologising, wasn't I? And I'll do it—I'll do it right, if it kills me. Fanny——"

"Ah, we'll take it as read, Tom," she said. "And when you meet Colin next in The Waggoners, I'd just forget the whole thing. Pretend it didn't happen."

"For Jean's sake, you mean?" he said.

"For Jean's sake," she agreed tactfully, thinking of peace, of peace at any price, as she had been enjoying it until the day when Kit had told her of his engagement to Laura Greenslade.

Looking at Sir Peter, she thought that he was another person who understood the value of peace. But she noticed now that he was no longer looking as calm and cheerful as he had a short time before. He was listening intently to Clare, who had got into one of her talking spells, but he was frowning and there was a distinct look of strain on his face. Fanny wondered what Clare could be saying that was making him look like that, and decided that later that evening she would insist on being told the reason for Clare's strange desire to meet him.

Only a few minutes later he got up to leave. His manner, as he said good-bye to Fanny and Basil, was oddly absent. He thanked them for a delightful evening, saying that he was particularly glad to have met Miss Forwood and particularly sorry to have missed meeting Mrs. Greenslade. But his mind, while he was speaking, seemed to be on something else.

Clare, still where he had left her, was staring musingly into space, even more lost to the world, for the moment, than

Sir Peter. From the doorway, in which he turned to look at
her once more, he gave her a little bow but she seemed not
even to see it.

Soon after Sir Peter had gone, Mrs. McLean left and soon
after her, the Mordues. Basil went out to the gate with them,
while Fanny stood in front of the old, gilt-framed mirror,
looking questioningly into the peculiarly lengthened, pallid
face that stared back at her out of the flawed glass. Basil,
returning, began at once to tidy the room.

" For God's sake, leave it! " Fanny exclaimed, as he started
collecting the glasses on to a tray. " Let's all have another
drink and forget the whole blasted show."

He took no notice of her but went on with his clearing and
straightening. Picking up the dish that had held the lobster
patties, on which there were only half a dozen left, he said,
" I should think these could go into the furnace, couldn't
they ? "

" I should think they could! " Fanny said. She took a look
at the dish. " Six! Only six left. Well, if he spends the night
being sick, he can't say I didn't warn him. I never saw anything so extraordinary in my life." She threw herself into a
chair. " Kit, get me another drink. Then you might go up
and see how Laura is. See if she's feeling well enough to
have dinner with us, or if she'd like something on a tray, or
what. And tell her that the lobster patties were wonderful
and that they all got eaten. You know . . ." She reached out
to take the glass that Kit had filled for her. " I can't think
why one actually bothers with food at all on these occasions.
People don't really want to eat, they only want drinks and
something for their hands to fiddle with. But it's a chance
for me to show off with one of the few things I can do well
so that's why I do it. But I'll never do it again, never." She
gulped her drink, leant back and closed her eyes.

Kit went out of the room. A faint crunching sound from
Clare's corner of the room told Fanny that she was eating
salted almonds.

Opening her eyes again, Fanny asked, " Well, did you get
what you wanted from the Poulter man ? "

" I didn't want anything from him," Clare replied.

" What did you want then? "

" Just to see what he was like."

" Oh come—there's got to be some reason for your interest in him."

" There is, of course. But that's really all I wanted—just to see what he was like."

" Did you tell him so? "

" What do you imagine? "

" I suppose you wouldn't—though I don't really see why not. But you must have said something to upset him."

" I? " Clare said in surprise.

Fanny nodded.

" What makes you think so? " Clare asked warily.

" His whole manner changed a little while before he left, and he wasn't talking to anyone but you, so I thought it must have been something you'd said to him."

" I don't think so," Clare said. " I really don't. I can't think of anything that could have. . . . Are you sure? "

" No, of course not, I don't know him well enough to be sure. Perhaps he was just bored at the whole thing and at that point stopped pretending not to be."

" Oh, I don't think he was bored," Clare said a little sharply.

" Well, are you going to see him again? " Fanny asked.

Clare looked irritated, as if she found that Fanny was asking too many questions.

" Probably," she said shortly.

" When? " Fanny persisted.

" I don't know. To-morrow perhaps. I'll tell you all about it some time, when I know a little more clearly what I think about it all myself."

" It's all very mysterious."

" Yes, isn't it ? "

" I liked him myself," Fanny said. " I hope we see some more of him."

" I expect you will."

But in this Clare was wrong. She was wrong in thinking that she would see Sir Peter next day or indeed that she or Fanny would ever see him again.

As he walked back to his house along the quiet village street, he was taken violently ill, and late in the night, in extreme pain, with Dr. McLean at his bedside, working uselessly to save his life, Sir Peter Poulter died.

CHAPTER SEVEN

DR. McLEAN was a small, slight, grey-haired man, curiously like his wife in appearance and manner. His skin was less sunburnt than hers, since he had less time to spend in the garden than she, but his face, like hers, was long and thin and deeply lined, with the same kind smile and clear blue gentle gaze.

However, he had not quite her capacity for concentrating his thoughts on only one thing, which meant that he had never quite achieved such serenity as hers. His narrow forehead sometimes wrinkled in a worried frown and the blue eyes became deeply troubled. Yet even at such times they seldom lost their look of sympathy. There was sympathy in them, as well as the shadow of a great tiredness and anxiety, as he told Fanny and Basil, on the morning after the death of Sir Peter Poulter, that he was not wholly satisfied as to the cause of that death.

Dr. McLean had come straight from Sir Peter's house to theirs and asked to see them alone. They had not yet had breakfast. Fanny, in an old quilted dressing-gown and with her hair more unkempt than usual, had been in the kitchen, yawning as she filled the electric kettle to make tea. Basil, fully dressed and as neat as ever, had been laying the fire in the sitting-room.

Because of Dr. McLean's insistence that he wanted to speak to them privately, they took him into the small room behind the antique shop, which was used by Fanny as an office. But no one else in the house was stirring yet. Only Spike took an interest in Dr. McLean's arrival. Pattering along the passage with his claws clicking on the stone flags, he sat down outside the closed door of the little office, scratching at it and whining to be let in. Dr. McLean wished that Fanny and Basil would either let the dog in or send him away. The soft little whines worked on the doctor's tired nerves so that they seemed to be almost the last straw after the terrible night.

Controlling himself, he watched the looks of shock and horror on the two faces before him. Fanny's face expressed the more, tears gathering quickly in her eyes and trickling unregarded down her cheeks. Basil's face became drawn and remote, with a look in the eyes which surprised the doctor. It was almost, he thought afterwards, a look of calculation.

It was Fanny who said in a shaking voice, " The lobster— it was that frightful lobster."

Dr. McLean closed his eyes for a moment, partly from exhaustion and partly to shut out the sight of what he saw dawning in her face.

" That's what I wanted to ask you about, my dear," he said. " I want you to tell me all about what Sir Peter had to eat and drink while he was here. Because, you see, he had nothing to eat after he got home. He was already feeling ill by the time he got in—in fact he had his first attack of vomiting by the garden gate."

" The lobster," Fanny repeated. It was plain that she was hardly listening to what he was saying. " I tried to stop him eating it. I knew there was something horribly wrong with it. But he said it was delicious and he would go on. . . . I couldn't understand it. None of us could, because it tasted awful."

" You mean you could actually taste that there was something wrong with it? " Dr. McLean asked.

" Taste it! " Fanny said. " No one else even tried to eat it."

" Yet Sir Peter liked it? "

" Yes, and he insisted on going on with it, even when I tried to take it away from him. I did try, Dr. McLean, I really did. They'll all tell you so. It must be my fault that poor man's dead—I must have got more absent-minded than usual and put some frightful thing into the sauce—but when

I tasted how awful it was I did try to take it away from him.
I didn't mean to do him any harm. I liked him. I thought
he was so——"

Basil interrupted her by pressing a hand on her shoulder.
" It wasn't your fault," he said. " Don't start saying that.
The lobster itself must have been bad."

" But then it would have tasted quite different," she said.
" In fact, with all those spices, it might have tasted perfectly
all right.   But that horrible bitter thing must have been
something that I put in, in mistake for the paprika or the
brandy or I don't know what."

" Bitter? " Dr. McLean said.

" Yes," Basil said, " it was very unpleasantly bitter."

" Yet Sir Peter liked it? "

" Yes."

" Isn't that very strange? "

" It is."

" And no one else besides Sir Peter liked it? "

" No one at all. In fact, I don't think anyone else swallowed
more than one mouthful."

" Then it looks as if the lobster probably was the cause of
the trouble," the doctor said. He spoke hesitantly, glancing
unhappily from one face to the other, then down at his own
hands.   " It's terribly sad, but—well, these things happen.
I know how you must be feeling, but don't blame yourselves.
No one could possibly think of blaming either of you. But I
think it would be a good thing, don't you, if I took some of
the remnants away with me for analysis? We may all feel
certain it was the lobster, but we'll have to make sure."

He waited for an answer. When none came, he looked up
again at the two faces before him. Fanny, he thought, might
not even have heard what he had said. She was staring
before her while the tears ran down her cheeks and splashed
from her chin on to the old quilted dressing-gown, making
wet blotches on the shabby material. But Basil, sitting on
the arm of her chair and with his hand still upon her
shoulder, was watching Dr. McLean with an unfamiliar
look of wariness in the bright, dark eyes that usually looked
so candid and innocent.

Outside in the passage Spike whined again and scratched impatiently at the door.

" Well? " Dr. McLean said, a little more abruptly.

" The trouble is," Basil said quietly, " there aren't any remnants."

" But you said——"

" I know, that most people left theirs. They did, and the sight was so unpleasant that I collected them all as soon as the party broke up and dumped the lot in the furnace. And later in the evening we washed up, so there aren't even any scraps left on plates or in the saucepan that Fanny used when she cooked the stuff."

" I see."

" It's unfortunate," Basil said.

" It is."

" But what difference does it make? " Fanny wailed suddenly. " We know it was the lobster and we know it was my fault. It's no good trying to tell me it wasn't. I invited that poor old man here and I gave him poison and killed him. I didn't mean to, but it feels just as bad as if I'd done it on purpose. I killed him by being careless and muddled and absent-minded, and that's as bad as doing it on purpose, and I don't know how I'm going to live with that thought in my mind now. I'm not going to be able to bear it. I never wanted to harm anyone and I shall go mad! "

" Quiet," Basil said. " We don't actually know that it was the lobster. But even if it was, we're quite sure it wasn't your fault." He turned back to Dr. McLean. " Aren't we? "

" Yes, yes," the doctor said uneasily. " In any case, it's very puzzling, if, as you say, the taste was so markedly unpleasant. It's possible, of course, that Sir Peter's sense of taste was defective. That can happen. In fact, it sounds the most probable explanation of the circumstances. I wish, all the same, that you had some of the scraps left over. And the glass that he drank out of, I'd have liked to have that. But that got washed up too, I suppose."

" I'm afraid so," Basil said.

" It's a pity. It might have simplified things later."

" Yes." Basil's hand had shifted from Fanny's shoulder to

her head, and was gently smoothing her ruffled grey hair, which seemed to have a soothing effect upon her, but his eyes had not left the doctor's. " McLean, just what are you so scared of? "

Dr. McLean started slightly. " Scared? " he said. " Yes, I suppose that's the word for it. Yes, I'm very scared. But I don't think I ought to say any more about it until I know more. That's why I wanted to talk to you quite privately. I'd hoped you might be able to tell me something. . . . But you can't, so that doesn't help."

" In other words," Basil said, " what's on your mind is something quite different from ordinary food-poisoning. You don't believe there was anything wrong with the lobster itself."

" Of course there wasn't," Fanny cried, suddenly jerking her head away from Basil's hand. " I've told you, it was something I put into it, or spilled over it. It was my doing, it was my fault."

Dr. McLean shook his head. It was a gesture of weariness and helplessness rather than of negation.

" At any rate, would you do something for me, my dear? " he said. " Don't go around saying that—not yet. And don't —don't tell anyone that I've been asking you these questions. I only came to ask them because I thought that—well, if we run into difficulties, it might have been helpful to know certain things."

" I think you're trying to tell us that you hoped you might be able to keep us out of trouble," Basil said. " We're very grateful."

The doctor shrugged. " I may be all wrong, remember. It's been a pretty bad night and I may be worrying unduly. But just tell me one thing—that bad taste, you're sure it was bitter? "

" Yes," Basil said.

" I don't understand it," Dr. McLean said with a sigh as he got up to go. " I can't think why it should have been bitter."

As he went out, Spike jumped up at him exuberantly, in ill-timed delight at seeing an old friend. The doctor tugged absently at the dog's ears, then, out in the garden, turned once more to Basil, who was following him to the gate.

" Really," he said, " don't let her go around saying it was her fault. You know how rumours can start."

Basil nodded. " I just wanted to thank you," he said. " Fanny's too upset to think of it. And I wanted to ask you, how long it will be before you know? "

" A few days."

" And if you're right? "

Dr. McLean gave the same headshake, the same tired, defeated gesture as he had given a few minutes before.

" Then it's out of my hands, you know. At the very least, it'll mean a good deal of unpleasantness." He made an attempt to summon his usual cheerfulness. " There's no point in your worrying before it happens, anyway. It isn't as if I can make any sense of the situation. Bitter. It really shouldn't have been bitter. That doesn't make sense."

Looking a little brighter, he walked off quickly to his car.

Basil waited a moment, looking after him, then went slowly back into the house.

He found Fanny still sitting in the little office, her elbows on the desk in front of her and her head in her hands. Her eyes were still swimming and her breathing sounded as if she had a bad cold.

" Come along," Basil said, " let's have some breakfast."

She nodded but did not stand up.

" Basil, what *is* he specially afraid of ? " she asked.

He hesitated, then answered in a low voice, " Arsenic, I think."

" *Arsenic?* " she nearly screamed. " He thinks I gave that poor old man *arsenic?* "

" No," Basil said. " But he's horribly afraid somebody did. Now let's go and get the breakfast."

She was frowning. " But arsenic isn't bitter. I thought it was tasteless."

" That's what's worrying him."

" The awfully bitter thing is strychnine, isn't it? "

" Yes—strychnine's bitter."

" But the symptoms would be quite different."

" Very different."

" And we've no arsenic in the house—or strychnine."

" I sincerely hope not."

Still frowning, she got slowly to her feet. She took a step towards the door, then suddenly reached out a hand to Basil and clasped one of his.

" I think I'm rather frightened," she said.

With a sigh he said, " These things shouldn't happen to one before one's had breakfast, should they? "

" I know, I know—I'm coming," she said. " Though I couldn't eat anything myself."

" And remember," he said, " when the others come down, don't tell them all you killed Sir Peter with arsenic. Don't tell them anything except that he's dead."

" I'll try. . . ." She gave a shiver. " But I'm not very good at hiding things, am I? And I *am* frightened. I'm getting more and more frightened every moment."

She went out to the kitchen, and with an occasional tear still running down her cheeks, put the kettle to boil and swstched on the hot-plates.

She had just made the tea, a few pieces of toast and boiled an egg for Basil, when Laura came down. It was almost shocking to Fanny to see Laura's cheerful face. It was a reminder that Laura, Clare and Kit would all have to be told of Sir Peter's death, a fact which Fanny, immersed in her own distress and mounting terror, had been forgetting.

Laura showed no signs this morning of having suffered from a bad headache. She looked fresh and lovely. She was wearing a simple dress of pale green jersey and flat-heeled country shoes, and with only a very little make-up on her face, looked younger and brighter than she had the day before. Seeing Fanny's blotched and tear-streaked face, she at once showed startled concern.

" Why, what's the matter? " she said, her voice warm and kind. " Whatever's happened? "

Fanny told her that Sir Peter was dead.

Laura gave a little gasp and said that she was terribly sorry to hear it.

Fanny genuinely had intended to tell her no more than

that simple fact, but at that point a new thought struck her and she exclaimed, " And how lucky you were to have that headache yesterday, because if you hadn't . . . But of course you wouldn't have eaten the stuff like he did, so you'd have been all right. No one else ate it, and why he should have when it tasted so horrible. . . . But I suppose we'll never understand that now. How is the headache, by the way? "

" Quite gone, thank you," Laura answered. " I wanted to tell you how sorry I was about it yesterday. It isn't often I get such bad ones as that, but when I do I'm quite helpless. But I am awfully sorry. To have it happen the very first time we met. . . . What did you mean, though, about its being lucky? I don't think I understood."

" Lucky you didn't try to eat the lobster that killed the Poulter man," Fanny said, beginning to cry again. " But it's all right, it wouldn't have harmed you, because you wouldn't have gone on eating it like he did. Everyone else left theirs, thank God! I'm not a mass murderer. But if only I knew what I'd done! "

Laura looked at her thoughtfully. She decided apparently that Fanny, in her present condition, was not likely to be able to tell a coherent story about Sir Peter's death, so giving a little murmur of sympathy, Laura merely waited.

After a moment, Fanny went on, " And I made the lobster things on purpose for you, and now I don't suppose I'll ever make them again."

" Then there was something wrong with the lobster, was there? " Laura asked. " He died of food-poisoning? "

" Yes," Fanny said quickly. " Food-poisoning."

" How really terrible for you," Laura said. " Or rather, for whoever sold you the lobster, because that's the person who's really to blame. It's often terribly difficult to guess that shell-fish isn't fresh, and some people ought never to eat it anyway, however much they like it. I expect Sir Peter was really one of those. I'm sure you shouldn't blame yourself at all."

Fanny gave her a grateful glance. " It's nice of you to say that. But I feel awful—*awful!* I never knew one could feel as awful as I feel."

" Of course you feel awful. Anyone would. But still I'm certain you aren't to blame," Laura said firmly.

Fanny started to say something but a fresh gush of tears stopped her. These tears were caused, not by the thought of Sir Peter's death, but by a sudden sense of intense gratitude to Fate for having found Kit such a really nice, good, kind wife. It felt wonderfully soothing to let these tears pour for a moment. Then Fanny came round the kitchen table and embraced Laura.

" Thank you," she said. " That's made me feel better. Lots better. Now tell me what you'd like for breakfast."

" I'm ravenous," Laura said simply.

Fanny, again all gratitude, felt that in the circumstances this was the kindest and most tactful answer possible.

A little while later she told the whole story again to Kit and then to Clare. With Kit Fanny spoke only briefly, for as soon as he had grasped the central fact that Sir Peter Poulter had died in the night, probably as a result of having eaten the lobster that Fanny had cooked, he went to Basil for the details of the story. But Clare questioned Fanny closely and lengthily. She discarded at once Fanny's faltering statement that presumably the lobster had not been fresh and asked her what it was that she really feared.

This Clare did partly because of the rather curious thing that she had found Fanny doing when she came into the kitchen.

Fanny, standing with her back to the door and unaware that she was being watched, had been taking down tins and bottles from a shelf, opening each in turn, jabbing a finger into its contents, then licking the finger. Clare stood and watched her for a moment, seeing Fanny shake her head several times and once hearing her mutter, " No, that *isn't* bitter."

" So you're conducting a post-mortem on the lobster, are you? " Clare said when she heard that.

Fanny turned with an exclamation.

" Post-mortem! " she cried. " Post-mortem! Lord, why did you have to say just that, of all things? That's what they've got to do."

After that Clare got the rest of the story easily.

Its effect on her appeared to be slight, except that her face became a little paler and more rigid than usual. Her quick, probing questions hastened the telling of the story. But when Fanny in her turn asked a question, Clare merely gave her a severe glance, turned on her heel and walked out of the kitchen.

Fanny's question had been: " Why *were* you so keen on getting to know him, Clare? "

Her refusal to answer did not much disturb Fanny. She knew Clare far too well to imagine that she could make her say anything that she did not want to say, and since Clare had already refused to answer this question, Fanny had hardly expected to obtain any information now. Turning back to the cupboard, she went on taking out tins of spices, packets of cake mixture and blanc manges and dried herbs, opening them, thrusting a finger-tip inside, tasting. Anything which had been within her reach the day before and which, in a truly exaggerated fit of absent-mindedness, she might have put into the sauce in which she had cooked the lobster, she tasted. But nothing in the cupboard tasted other than how it should have tasted. Nothing tasted unduly bitter.

CHAPTER EIGHT

CLARE AND LAURA returned to London in the afternoon. Clare had a rooted objection to driving in the dark, and in spite of the persuasions of Fanny and Basil, she insisted on leaving them soon after lunch. She always allowed herself far longer than she needed for any journey, still feeling in her heart, after many years of driving, that she was not really capable of inducing her car to arrive at her destination.

But the persuasions that day had not been very pressing. Even Kit, who suggested to Laura that she should stay the night and let Basil drive her back to London early the next morning, seemed almost relieved when she shook her head and said that she would travel with Miss Forwood.

Kit and Laura had been out for a walk together during the morning. It was a fine morning, with the sky a little hazy, suggesting that the sun would shine brightly later and with the soft, exciting sense of spring in the air. Yet when Kit and Laura returned they were both quiet and subdued. Whether this was a gesture of deference on their part to death and to Fanny's brooding misery, or whether it was simply the house and the presence of other people that affected them in this way, Clare did not know, but she noticed a half-smothered irritability develop in Kit, an air of feeling deeply though confusedly resentful at the way that life was treating him.

Laura took an affectionate farewell of Fanny, who responded vaguely. She seemed to be hardly aware of the girl, or of Clare or Kit. Though she clung to Basil, as if he were the only person who could help her to face her own thoughts, she spent a good deal of time in a frowning silence, with the look of someone who was struggling with some problem that was quite beyond her mental capacity.

In the car on the way back to London, Laura remarked, " Fanny is a wonderful person, isn't she? But isn't it curious how different people are from what one expects? Kit had given me a completely wrong idea of her, yet I suppose he thought he was telling me the truth."

" In what way was it wrong? " Clare asked.

" Well, I never thought she'd be such a—such a simple sort of person," Laura said.

" She isn't simple at all," Clare replied.

" Oh, I think she is—a really good-hearted, simple person. I liked her even more than I thought I was going to."

" She *is* good-hearted," Clare said.

" It's a tremendous load off my mind," Laura went on, " that we got on so well, even in those terrible circumstances. because, you know, until we met, I was just a little afraid that . . . well, that I should have to have a fight with her. And that would have been a pity."

" And now you think you can get what you want without a fight? " Clare said.

Her tone made Laura glance at her doubtfully, but Clare's

face expressed nothing but nervous concentration on her driving.

" Oh, I'm sure of it," Laura said. " She isn't at all a selfish or domineering person—and honestly, that's what I was a bit afraid of. Though everything Kit said about her was complimentary, I had somehow the fear, that she was going to be possessive and difficult about Kit and would hate me if I stood up to her. But I'm absolutely sure now that she isn't like that at all."

" And so Kit and you are going to live in London, are you? " Clare said. " It's all arranged? "

" Arranged? " Laura said, and for some reason her colour deepened. " We hardly even discussed it. But knowing Fanny now, I know it's going to turn out all right."

" Kit wants to go, does he? "

" Of course." There was a slight sharpness in Laura's voice as she said it.

" Well, I'm sure you're right to insist on it," Clare said, hoping that the subject might be dropped. To have spent, out of more than twenty-four hours, only the few precious hours of sleep by herself, and during the rest of the time to have endured what she considered an almost shocking amount of emotional experience, was something that at any time would have produced in her a mood of acute dislike of other human beings. She was feeling at that moment an almost physical lust to be alone. If that was impossible, then the next best thing would be silence.

But Laura went on, " You know, if I could have helped at all, I'd have stayed on, but I got the feeling that Fanny and Basil wanted to be on their own. I do hope I was right. D'you think I was? "

" Probably," Clare said.

" But I still don't understand what actually happened yesterday."

" I don't think anybody does."

" I didn't like to press Fanny for details," Laura said, " because she was obviously so upset, but I can't help puzzling over it. Kit said that there was something wrong with the lobster and that nobody but Sir Peter ate any of it."

" Yes, that's what happened."

" But why did he eat it? "

" He said it was delicious."

" But if everyone else——"

" I know, I know—*why?* " Clare broke in, suddenly fierce,
making the car leap ahead wildly for an instant, then rear
back on its haunches. " Why did the silly old man insist on
eating the things when everyone told him they were bad?
Why couldn't he do the same as other people? He'd be alive
now if he had. Why do people have to do these ridiculous
things that only make trouble for other people? "

Laura gave her a thoughtful look, her eyebrows lifting a
little, as if she disliked the tone of these remarks. But she went
on pertinaciously with her inquiry. " The lobster actually
tasted so unpleasant that other people wouldn't eat it? "

" Yes."

" Yet Sir Peter said it was delicious and ate a lot of it? "

" Yes."

" But isn't that quite extraordinary? "

Clare did not reply. She was beginning to feel nervous of
what she might say if she spoke. Scowling ferociously at the
road, she wondered whether she might not find it useful in
her life to suffer from deafness. But this thought immediately
produced a superstitious fear in her. She had noticed, or
thought she had noticed, that if she thought of an illness, she
was almost immediately attacked by it. To ward off this
danger and show that she had heard Laura's question perfectly well, she gave a non-committal grunt.

" Did you taste the lobster? " Laura asked.

Clare grunted again.

" But whatever did it taste like?

" Bitter."

" Bitter? Just bitter? It tasted——"

There Laura stopped. She stopped with a little catch of
her breath, while one of her hands, lying in her lap, gave a
jerk and seemed to lift itself automatically a few inches, as if
some nerve had been struck.

There was silence for nearly a minute, then, in a soft,
careful voice, as if she were making an effort to keep all

expression out of it, Laura said, " You're quite sure that the lobster tasted *bitter?* "

The change in her way of speaking was so noticeable that Clare dared for an instant to shift her gaze from the road and snatch a glance at the girl beside her.

She found that Laura was staring at her with a fixed, intent look, her eyes unusually wide open and her face very pale. The way she was sitting had changed too, although she had not moved. Instead of looking relaxed and comfortable, she had become rigid.

" Yes," Clare said, her curiosity aroused. " It was very, very bitter."

But now, just when she would have liked Laura to go on talking, explaining the strange emotion that the thought of bitter-tasting lobster caused in her, Laura became silent and slowly turning her head away and looking out of the window beside her, so that Clare could not have seen her face even if she had looked at it again, did not even reply when Clare presently inquired, " Does that mean something to you? "

Laura scarcely spoke again before they reached London. The rigidity slowly went out of her body, but she then sat in a slumped and exhausted way, as if she were suffering the after-effects of a shock. After a while she complained that another of her headaches was developing and supporting her head on one hand, she covered her eyes.

Clare felt almost as irritated by this change as she had at Laura's earlier inquisitiveness. More than once she tried to draw her into talk, but all her attempts were failures. When they reached the block of flats where Laura lived and Laura got out of the car, turning at last to look at Clare and thank her for the drive, Clare saw that her eyes still had a fixed, empty look, as if her whole mind were occupied with thoughts that she did not mean to risk revealing.

But as Clare drove on to her own flat, she forgot about Laura, for as soon as she found herself alone, the thoughts that had been obstructed in her own mind by the mere presence of another person, began to flow with a feverish speed that washed away all interest in what did not just then immediately concern herself. She had plenty of thinking to do about the week-end. She had many things to sort out, many things about which she must come to some conclusion.

Next day she attempted to do some work. But she was wholly unsuccessful. Everything that she wrote she tore up. It was the same on the day following. The trouble was not merely that problems unrelated to what she was trying to write kept crowding into her mind, but that she felt incessantly that she was waiting for something. It hardly seemed worth her while to concentrate fully on anything, because it seemed certain to her that as soon as she did, she would be interrupted.

She did not clarify to herself what form she expected the interruption to take, but when it did not come and the hours passed without any disturbance of her quiet solitude in her Hampstead flat, she began to feel an unbearable suspense. The longer the time that passed, the more compelling became her conviction that some terrible thing was about to happen. The future seemed dreadful and her life shadowed by disaster.

At last, four days after her return to London, the interruption came and at once, although the event was sufficiently grim, Clare felt better. She had great skill in detaching herself from reality, once she knew what the reality was. Her voice, as she listened to Fanny's hurried and desperate speech on the telephone, was calm and unexcited.

" So it *was* arsenic ? " she said.

" Yes—and enough of it to kill a horse! " Fanny's voice reached her wildly. " Dr. McLean told me how many grains it was, but that didn't mean anything to me, so I asked him was that an awful lot and he answered that it was enough to kill a horse! "

" But isn't arsenic tasteless ? " Clare's question sounded like a pedantic insistence on accuracy.

" Yes, I'm sure it is," Fanny answered. " But they don't seem to be worrying much about that. They——"

" They ? " Clare interrupted.

" The police, of course," Fanny said. " They've been here all day, asking questions and questions and questions. And Clare——" Her voice stopped for an instant. " I think they'll be coming to see you."

" Yes, I rather expected that," Clare said.

" Of course I didn't tell them anything about your having specially asked me to arrange a meeting with the Poulter man. . . . Oh God, how I wish I hadn't! I just said you were a very old friend whom we'd asked down to help celebrate Kit's engagement. But Mrs. McLean told her husband that you and Sir Peter spent most of the evening talking together and I suppose he told the police and they asked a lot of questions about you and whether you'd ever met Sir Peter before and all that sort of thing. I just went on saying I didn't know anything about it at all—which of course is quite true. And as soon as I could get to the telephone I did, to warn you to expect them."

" I see," Clare said. " Thank you, Fanny." A sense of cold had suddenly slid down her spine, but her voice did not change. " Thank you very much. I gather they think it's murder."

" I think they think so," Fanny said, "except that they're trying to find out how I could have done it by accident. But there just isn't any arsenic in the house."

" And they're quite certain the arsenic was in the lobster? "

" No, of course they aren't. They can't be. It might have been in one of his drinks, or in a stuffed olive or anything— though I don't know if you could put enough arsenic into a stuffed olive to kill a horse. Perhaps it would take spoonfuls —I just don't know."

" And what about the inquest? "

" It's the day after to-morrow. I expect you'll have to come down for it. And so will Laura. The Mordues and the McLeans all remembered the Poulter man's saying that he remembered her and I think Tom's told the police all about it, with knobs on."

" But is there any certainty whatever that Sir Peter got the poison at your house? " Clare asked.

" I suppose there isn't—no absolute certainty, anyway. But his servants say he'd had nothing to eat or drink at home later than lunch-time, and if he'd had that huge dose of arsenic then, the symptoms would have come on much sooner."

" Suppose he had it after he left."

"Well, so far as anyone knows, he went straight home and he was taken ill before he even got into the house. And d'you remember how suddenly he left and how his manner changed. I thought at the time that you'd said something that had upset him, but now I realise that he must have been feeling ill and wanting to get away before anything happened."

"And suicide isn't even being considered?"

"I suppose they're considering everything, but . . ." The telephone was silent.

"I see—yes, they think it's murder," Clare said. "Well, thanks for warning me, Fanny."

"Oh, but I don't mean they're going to suspect you!" Fanny cried. "I don't think they've started to suspect anyone yet. They seem to think he was a man who had lots of enemies. I suppose people who make big fortunes always have. That's to say, they must be pretty ruthless sometimes, even when they're very pleasant to meet. And I dare say there were women too. He gave me that sort of feeling, in spite of his age. So there's no need for you to be in the least afraid of the police when they come, because apart from anything, the man I saw seemed to be quite reasonably intelligent and not at all likely to rush off madly after ridiculous ideas. But I know you don't like surprises, or strangers turning up unexpectedly and so on. That's why I rang you up at once, not because I thought they're going to suspect you. Personally, I should think they'd be much more likely to suspect Laura. In the light of after events, that headache of hers looks to me just a little suspicious. But naturally I haven't said a thing to turn their thoughts in that direction. I still believe that I'm responsible—though I haven't the faintest idea how I did it. Good-bye now, Clare. Let me know what happens."

"Yes," Clare said. "Yes, of course."

She put the telephone down. But she did not remove her hand from it, indeed the grasp of her fingers tightened round it. Sitting there, gazing absently at the wall before her, she kept a hold on the instrument as if it were a buoy on the end of a line that linked her to safety.

CHAPTER NINE

THE POLICE called on Clare the next day. A detective-inspector and a sergeant from Scotland Yard arrived together and spent about an hour with her. Before they came, she had thought out carefully the limit of what she meant to tell them. Their questions did not probe beyond this limit and so she talked, for her, fairly freely.

" No," she said in answer to a question as to whether or not she had ever met Sir Peter before the occasion of the Lynams' cocktail party, " I had never met him. But I wanted to meet him. I had even asked Mrs. Lynam to arrange a meeting with him for me, if she found herself able to do so."

She had decided on making this admission readily. This was not because she doubted that Fanny had said nothing to the police of her request concerning Sir Peter, but because it seemed almost certain that Fanny, before the day of the party, would have spoken to a number of people of Clare's uncharacteristic desire to meet a man who had owned a string of newspapers and that these people would not now forget that.

" I did not really expect Mrs. Lynam to arrange the meeting," she went on, speaking primly and distantly, while her big, deep-set eyes under the heavy forehead that over-shadowed the rest of her small, lined face, bored steadily but in fact rather blindly into the eyes of the inspector. " At the time I spoke of it she had never even spoken to Sir Peter, so I was hardly serious in making the request. But then she telephoned me one morning to say that she had met him and she invited me down for the week-end so that I could make his acquaintance."

" Was there any special reason why you wished to meet him? " the inspector asked.

" Yes," Clare said, " but it will be a rather difficult reason to explain."

In her own ears her manner of speaking sounded pedantic and false, betraying obviously how fully she had rehearsed her answers, but she hoped that to the two policemen it would seem a quite normal way for a nervous little old maid of literary leanings to speak.

" You see," she said carefully, " I am a writer."

The inspector nodded.

" I write novels," she said.

He nodded again.

" And sometimes," she said with a small, tight-lipped, deprecatory smile, " I find my characters quite a problem. I find I do not know nearly enough about them—about their backgrounds, their professions, the day-to-day details of their way of living. I myself live, you see, in a very secluded way. I really know very little indeed about the world."

" Ah," the inspector said, " then you mean you wanted to use Sir Peter as a character in one of your novels? "

She nodded brightly.

" Yes, I'm just planning a novel which concerns a news-paper proprietor," she said, " and when Mrs. Lynam chanced to remark to me that Sir Peter Poulter had come to live in their neighbourhood, I told her that it would really be most useful to me if I could meet him—most useful." She paused. " But now I shall never write the book."

To her own ears what she was saying sounded fantastic nonsense. Fanny had been right when she said that Clare never wrote about anything but her own family. Clare had never felt that she knew any other people sufficiently well to write about them, and besides that, no others had ever been sufficiently important to her for her to want to write about them. Over and over again in her work, she had grappled with the same characters and the same problems. Varying the plot that contained them only a trifle, she had always tried to reach a little deeper under the surface, groping her way closer to some ultimate answer which she felt, with quietly indignant doggedness, was owed to her by life.

However, there were, she believed, other ways of working. Writers existed, she had heard, though she found it a little hard to believe in them, who did arrange to meet unfamiliar types of person in order to study how they pronounced or mispronounced their words, ate their food and cracked their finger-joints, while some writers actually went expensive journeys in order to be able to describe accurately the backgrounds which they had mysteriously decided were appropriate to their stories. At the least, the lay public believed that writers did this kind of thing, and the police, it was to be hoped, were part of the lay public.

Just so long as this inspector did not turn out to be one of those utterly unexpected people who for reasons that she had never been able to comprehend, apparently found great pleasure in working slowly and painstakingly through the products of her curious imagination. . . .

If he was, he appeared to have no difficulty in concealing the fact. He nodded, as if he found her explanation perfectly convincing.

"Did Mrs. Lynam mention to you how she made Sir Peter's acquaintance?" he asked.

"Yes," Clare said. "But I believe the fact is that I know more about that than she does. Mrs. Lynam is such a friendly and unself-conscious person that it would never occur to her to look for reasons for the friendliness of other people. But Sir Peter, I believe, was not at all a naturally friendly man. He had great skill with other people, but was not genuinely genial or accessible. From what he told me, I'm sure that he made Mrs. Lynam's acquaintance with a purpose."

The inspector looked interested.

Clare went on, "His purpose was simply to be invited into that house. It was, you see, the house in which he had been born. His origins, you know, were very humble. His parents kept a small shop—the shop in which Mrs. Lynam now sells her antiques. And the house, during his childhood, was divided into two cottages. His parents occupied one of them. And he had felt a great desire, so he told me, to see his old home again."

"He told you this, but did not tell Mrs. Lynam?" the inspector said.

"Yes," she said. "But he would certainly have told Mrs. Lynam later."

" If he had not started to feel ill and left the party rather abruptly? "

" We don't know that he left the party because he was feeling ill," she said.

" Quite true," he said. " But that seems to have been the general impression of the people who were there."

" It's their impression now," she said, " after the event. At the time I don't think such a thought occurred to anyone."

" What was your own impressions at the time? " he asked.

" I think I took for granted that he had suddenly recollected that he was expected at home for some reason—his usual dinner-hour, for instance."

" And during the time that you were talking together, he seemed to you quite normal? "

" So far as I can guess what his normal behaviour was. He showed no signs of undue depression, if that's what you mean. He talked in a most interesting way and was charming to everybody."

He went on then to ask her what she could tell him about the lobster patties.

She told him that they were a speciality of Fanny's, and that she was peculiarly proud of her ability to make them. When she had said that much, Clare hesitated. Then she spoke of the pronounced bitter taste of the lobster on the evening of the party and the strangeness of Sir Peter's being unable to taste it.

" Some people, of course, like bitter flavours," she said, " but this was too extreme. No one could have liked it."

" So everyone else who tasted it has told me," the inspector said.

" I don't know what it can have been," Clare said. " It didn't remind me of anything I knew. It was just bitter."

" Can you tell me something else," the inspector said. " Who handled the dish with the lobster patties on it? "

" Besides Mrs. Lynam, you mean? "

" Yes."

" I did."

She thought he made a small movement of increased

attention. He said, " When you were sitting beside Sir Peter? "

" No, it was I who brought them in from the kitchen, just as Sir Peter was arriving."

" You were helping Mrs. Lynam? "

" Yes, she'd gone upstairs to lie down for a little. She was tired, so Mr. Lynam and I got things ready."

"Then Mr. Lynam handled the dish too? "

" Not just then. Earlier, I think, in the kitchen. But it was I who brought it into the sitting-room. You've probably been told, however, that the patties were simply left on the kitchen table for quite a long time. Anyone who watched for the right moment could have gone in, even from outside, through the back door. But tell me, Inspector, is there actually any evidence that the poison was in the lobster? "

He replied guardedly that he was exploring all possibilities, then went on, in only slightly different words, to ask Clare all the questions that he had already asked her.

This took her by surprise. She had been assuming that he was an intelligent man who would not need to be told a thing twice over. Then all of a sudden she recognised, with a flash of anger at her own stupidity, that the repetition was deliberate.

This made her extremely nervous, not because she was afraid that her second answers might contradict her first, but because it seemed to imply that she was actually under suspicion. Her voice grew a little hoarse, while her manner took on an added shade of hauteur and reserve. From an appearance of almost meek and retiring gentility, she changed to one of formidable severity. She began to look at the inspector, of whom she was now feeling wildly frightened, as if he were the least intelligent boy in her class.

Smoothly and quietly he changed his tactics. Leaning back in his chair and relaxing, as if the important part of the interview were now over, he said, " I wonder if the same thing has struck you about all this, Miss Forwood, as struck me as soon as I began to make inquiries as to what had actually happened that evening."

She said nothing, but sat there looking prepared to be intensely critical of any suggestion that he might make.

" I find the whole situation," he said, " somehow a little—how shall I say it?—well, lopsided."

She raised her untidy eyebrows in a question.

" Put it like this," he went on. " We have a group of people gathered together to celebrate a certain engagement. These people for the most part know each other well and it appears that there are certain—how shall I say it?—tensions, animosities almost, between them. Some serious, perhaps, some not so serious. What's serious and what isn't is very hard to judge until one has some real knowledge of the people involved. A father's rage, for instance, because he believes his daughter has been jilted, a woman's rage because she fears her son—actually her half-brother, of course, but in fact almost a son—is to be taken away from her, another woman's rage because she thinks her husband has been insulted. . . . Any one of these feelings might be serious or trivial according to the general make-up of the person in question. Don't you agree? "

The turn the conversation had taken surprised Clare agreeably.

" Of course I agree," she said. " But none of these things has anything to do with Sir Peter."

" And that's why I called the situation lopsided," the inspector said. " Here we have this group of people amongst whom—how shall I say it?—motives for murder might be discovered. Yet the person who dies is a person who apparently has no close connection with any other person there."

" Are you trying to tell me," Clare said, " that the person who got the poison wasn't the one who was meant to get it? "

" Oh no," he said, " certainly not that. I'm not even saying at this point that anyone was meant to get the poison. Accident really makes rather more sense of the evidence than murder does, or else perhaps—how shall I put it?——"

" In the first words that come into your head! " Clare suddenly snapped, his verbal mannerism doing more to shatter her self-control than anything that he had asked her.

He inclined his head slightly, as if in thanks for the advice.
" Malice, then," he said.   " That's what I was going to
say.   An ugly but not actually murderous malice, directed,
of course, against Mrs. Lynam."

Clare's forehead wrinkled.   This was an idea that had not
once occurred to her and she found it interesting.   She leant
a little forward.

" I think I see what you mean," she said.   " Someone may
have wanted to humiliate her and just because she was known
to be so proud of the way that she cooked lobster, deliberately
spoiled it for her.   All the same, surely using arsenic for the
purpose was going a little far ? "

" A little, yes.   But suppose that amount of arsenic had
been shared out among all the guests at the party instead of
being consumed almost entirely by one.   Everyone would
have had an unpleasant night and said that it was something
they had had at the party, probably Mrs. Lynam's lobster.
But no one would have died."

" But the bitter taste, Inspector ! "

" Yes, I agree that makes it complicated."   He gave a
sigh.   " Yet that might have been an accident, after all.
Mrs. Lynam herself seems to think that she can sometimes
act so absent-mindedly that she might easily have used some
quite inappropriate ingredient by mistake."

" And then just the one man in the neighbourhood who
can't taste that ingredient, whatever it was, comes to the
party and eats up all the lobster patties by himself.   Isn't that
just a bit too much of a coincidence, Inspector ? "

" It would be a coincidence, certainly.   And yet it's a very
important thing in my sort of work to remember that—how
shall I say it?—well, coincidences do happen.   One's inclined,
of course, to look for a pattern in everything and to refuse to
believe in the purely chance occurrence.   But that can be a
great mistake.   Yes, a great mistake."

" And how will you test your theory? " Clare asked.
" How will you find out if there's any truth in it ? "

" Only by tracing the source of the poison."

Soon after that the inspector and the sergeant left.   Clare
felt that an ordeal was over and for the moment was so relieved

by the feeling that she put out of her mind the thought that there would certainly be more interviews, more ordeals.

Sitting down at her desk, she picked up her pen and started to stare absorbedly at a sheet of paper.

Half an hour later the sheet of paper was still blank and some of the sense of peace and security had evaporated. Against her will and against the rigorous discipline that she was usually able to impose on her mind, she found it thronged with distracting images of a group of people in most of whom, she assured herself, she had next to no genuine interest.

The Mordues, for instance, and horse-faced, garden-loving Mrs. McLean, and the excitable young woman with the delicate flushed face, who had burst into the kitchen, carrying an armful of almond blossom, and her husband who had been so insulted, but whom Clare had not yet seen.

What did any of them matter to her? What, in a sense, did even Sir Peter Poulter mean to her?

Sighing, she pushed her chair back. At that moment her door-bell rang.

At any other time she would probably not have answered it. If the sheet of paper on her desk had had even a line or two written upon it, the bell could have rung again and again and Clare would not have stirred. But now, almost glad of the interruption, she actually hurried to the door.

Outside she found Laura Greenslade. She greeted Clare with an artificial smile and mechanical-sounding apologies for disturbing her, and when Clare invited her to come in, walked in with her head held unnaturally high and her whole body oddly stiff. It was the walk, and her voice had been the voice, of a person desperately controlling some violent emotion.

In the brighter light of her sitting-room, meeting Laura's china-blue eyes, Clare knew at once what the emotion was. It was the emotion of which she knew so much. It was fear. Laura was in a state of panic which might erupt at any moment into screaming hysteria.

Becoming rigid with resistance to the infection of the feeling, Clare did not speak, but left it all to Laura.

Standing quite still in the middle of the room, her arms

hanging straight at her sides, Laura said in a thin, high voice, " You've heard, haven't you? "

" Yes," Clare said.

" About the arsenic? "

" Yes."

" And you know—you know, don't you, who did it? "

" I certainly do not."

" But you must know! "

" I know nothing whatever about it, Mrs. Greenslade." Clare's voice was empty and cold, not angry or excited, but simply toneless.

Laura drew a trembling breath, and her big blue eyes, bright with the abnormal glitter of terror, searched Clare's face.

At last she said, " Perhaps you don't. Perhaps you don't understand what was meant to happen. After all, you don't know about me, do you? "

" It's true, I don't know much about you," Clare replied.

" They didn't tell you—the Lynams? "

" Since I don't know what you're referring to . . ."

" Oh, you'd know if they had. And you'd have realised at once that it wasn't Sir Peter Poulter who was meant to die. That was just an accident. They meant to kill me, Miss Forwood."

" They? The Lynams? " Clare's voice was angry now and there was a scowl on her heavy forehead.

" Of course! " Laura cried, her stiffness suddenly vanishing and her whole body beginning to tremble violently. " And I can prove it—because, you see, there's something peculiar about me and the Lynams know it. Fanny and Basil—they know all about it. And that's why they thought they were safe to try and kill me like that."

" Peculiar? " Clare said. The word stirred a memory of something that Basil had said.

" Yes—awfully peculiar," Laura said. " Awfully."

" But what is this peculiarity? "

" *I can't taste phenylthiourea!* "

CHAPTER TEN

THERE WAS anti-climax in it for Clare. The statement was so meaningless to her that at first hearing it seemed impossible that it could in fact have meaning for anyone.

Sitting down, folding her hands in her lap and looking sternly at Laura, she waited for a repetition of the gibberish, or an explanation.

Laura looked dazed for a moment, as if to her it were astonishing that explanations could be necessary. Then sitting down too, she said carefully, " Phenylthiourea is an organic compound which is intensely bitter. About one person in four is unable to taste it in concentrations of about fifty parts per million. They can, however, frequently taste it if raised in concentration to four hundred parts per million." Her voice changed, losing the sound of a repeated lesson. " Only very unusual people can't taste it at all! Only one in thousands and thousands! "

" And how," Clare inquired with great detachment, " does one set about finding out if one is one of these unusual people? "

She did not mean to be callous. She could see the girl's terror, and fear was an emotion with which in theory she had great sympathy. But contact with it roused something in herself that scared her so much that she struggled instantly to repress it.

" It happened to me when I was at the university," Laura said a little more quietly. " Basil Lynam was doing some sort of genetical experiment. He wanted students to come and taste various things and I was one of the ones who volunteered. There were hundreds of us, but I was the only one who couldn't taste the stuff at all."

" This phenol . . .? "

" Phenylthiourea."

" And so you think Basil remembered this about you? "

" Of course."

Clare feared that this at least was true.

" It all sounds very complicated and unlikely," she said.

" Not to him, he's a scientist," Laura said. " It'd be quite natural for him to think of something like that."

" To think of it, possibly, but hardly to do it."

Laura's body jerked in a long shiver. " It was Fanny who did it—or made him do it."

" That hardly makes it less unlikely," Clare said. " As I understand it, what you're saying is that Basil and Fanny, for some mysterious reason, decided to kill you—though Fanny had never even seen you and Basil's contact with you had been slight——"

" But there's nothing mysterious about it, Miss Forwood, nothing! " Laura cried. " You can see how Fanny is about Kit, can't you? He's the child she never had. He's the object of all her strongest emotions. She hates me, not because of what I am, but because of Kit's love for me. I threaten her very existence."

" But in the car you told me—— "

" That was before I knew about the phenylthiourea. I'd let her deceive me."

" Very well," Clare said patiently. " You're saying then that Fanny has such a possessive love for Kit that she was filled with murderous hatred of the woman whom he had decided to marry, that she discussed this with her husband, and that he either shared her feelings sufficiently or is so completely dominated by her—— "

" He is, he is, that's easy to see! "

" He's so completely dominated by her then, that he was ready to supply her with a strange and ingenious method of murdering you, together with the peculiar chemical and presumably the arsenic also, that were required by this method. And this method consisted of poisoning a quantity of food which was going to be offered to a number of people, not only to you, by adding something which would make it taste so unpleasant to everyone but you that there was no risk of anyone but you eating enough of the food to be even taken ill."

Laura nodded her head several times. "That's it—that's it exactly."

"But heavens above!" Clare said. "Don't you see what you're suggesting? If you were right that Fanny and Basil are so insane and cruel that they could act in this way against you, that would be terrible enough. But what you're saying is that when they knew that you had been attacked by one of your bad headaches and were not going to come to the party, they could still go on and offer this poisoned dish to their friends. Not only that, but you believe that when they saw that one of their other guests actually had this same idiosyncracy as you and that he was prepared to eat spoonfuls of phenol—phenyl——"

"Phenylthiourea."

"Yes—to eat spoonfuls of it with relish, so that he was certain to get all the arsenic intended for you, they were ready to let him do this."

"They're mad," Laura said. "Quite mad. At least, Fanny is. She probably enjoyed watching poor Sir Peter taking the poison. After all, if she was mad enough to try to kill me in that way, she was mad enough for the other too —mad and evil."

"Evil?" Clare said thoughtfully. It was the sort of word that embarrassed her. "Well now, putting the question of evil aside, what about probability? I mean mathematical probability, about which I'm sure you know far more than I do. If an inability to taste this substance with the difficult name is really as unusual as you tell me, then wasn't it improbable in the extreme that two people with this inability should actually be in the same small house in the same small village at the same time?"

"Of course, of course," Laura said, striking the arms of her chair with the palms of her hands. "It's almost incredible. But it isn't impossible. Don't you see? There was only a chance of it in thousands—but there *was* a chance. You could calculate the improbability of it, but you'd still have to say that it *could* happen."

"All the same, it would be an amazing coincidence."

" But coincidences do · happen—the most amazing co-incidences! "

Remembering what the detective-inspector had said about coincidences, Clare nodded unwillingly. He had said that it could be a great mistake to look for a pattern in everything, and that coincidences did happen. That was what was always said about them. Coincidences do happen. She gave a sigh.

" Yes," she said, " of course they do, though it's annoying of them sometimes. I suppose we've got to accept it as a fact that there's at least some bitter substance that neither you nor Sir Peter Poulter could taste, though most other people found it overpoweringly strong. I certainly did. But I'm perfectly convinced that Fanny and Basil would never try to poison you—or anybody—in that way of all ways and that you've nothing whatever to fear from them. This talk of ours has made me quite sure that if a murder of any sort was intended by anyone, then Sir Peter was always to have been the victim. The coincidence was that *you* should have been in the house, not that *he* should have been."

Laura made a curious little grimace. She appeared to think that Clare was putting her in her place, reminding her that Sir Peter was a person of rather more note than herself.

" You just don't understand," she said. " I'm sorry— I thought you would. That's why I came."

" I at least understand Fanny Lynam a great deal better than you do," Clare said. " I know that she isn't a murderess. There's a lot more of the murderess in me than there is in her."

Laura stood up. She gave a faint smile and a faint shake of the head, as if in a half-secret mockery of Clare's limitations.

" Shall I tell you what I really thought about Fanny? " she said. " Shall I tell you how she really struck me with her creepy old house and her dog and her cat and her terrible clothes and that awful mirror in her sitting-room, that takes all the colour out of one's face and makes one look like a corpse? "

" You told me in the car that you liked her," Clare reminded her.

Laura repeated her small, secret smile.   It struck Clare this time as malicious and dangerous.

" Do you always say just what you really think? " Laura asked.   " The truth is that I thought her the nearest thing to an authentic witch that I'd ever met.   And I can just see her brewing her horrible potions over the fire."

An angry laugh broke from Clare.   " You have a very vivid imagination," she said.   " I don't think you thought of that until this moment.   And there's one thing you haven't told me yet.   Where does Kit stand in all this? "

" Of course he knows nothing about it," Laura answered.

" He doesn't even know that you can't taste that bitter stuff? "

" Not unless Basil or Fanny mentioned it."

" Yet there must be a lot of people who know that fact about you."

Laura frowned.   " I don't think so.   How could there be? "

" What about all the other people who were guinea-pigs for the same experiment? "

" Oh, but——" Laura paused, then shook her head. " That was years ago," she said, dismissing the suggestion. " I don't see any of them now.   And certainly none of them was at Fanny's party.   No—however much you may dislike the idea, Miss Forwood, I think you can be sure that it was Basil Lynam who remembered that fact about me."

" Which brings us back to that other fact, that it was Sir Peter who died and not you, and that there's still no certain proof of how he got the poison that killed him."

Laura gave an impatient shrug and turned towards the door.   Clare was relieved to see her ready to go and said nothing to keep her, yet even as she followed her out of the room and then closed the hall door upon her, she was haunted by the feeling of having failed to say something to her that was of great importance.

It was only after some minutes of confused and angry recapitulation to herself of the whole interview that she realised what it was that she had forgotten to say.   She had forgotten to ask Laura what she intended to do next with her suspicions.

This realisation sent Clare to the telephone. She rang up Fanny, told her that certain important matters had come up and that she was coming down to see her again that same day.

She went by train, because of her dislike of driving in the dark. Basil met her at the station. He seemed to Clare to be quite his usual self and to be showing no signs that Sir Peter's death and questioning by the police and the possibility that he, his wife or one of his friends might be suspected of murder, were more difficult to bear than any of the little everyday ills of life.

But still, as Clare knew, with Basil you never could tell. In his kind and friendly way, he was one of the most self-contained people she had ever known. He was concerned now that she might be tired and that she must be worried and was putting herself out on Fanny's account. When Clare suggested that all these things might be said of him, too, he only smiled quite cheerfully and shook his head.

" Our trouble is Kit," he said, and laughed, as if Kit, as a matter of course, were a subject of humour. " Kit in love —or perhaps not in love. I find I have a certain wish that he would make up his mind about it."

" He seemed to me to be very much in love," Clare said.

" That was last Saturday."

" Is he as inconstant as that, then ? "

" I'm not sure. But something in his life isn't as simple as he thought it was going to be."

" Well, presumably he was unprepared for a case of arsenical poisoning at his engagement party."

" No, poor boy. But I have a suspicion his troubles go deeper."

She gave him a curious look. " Deeper than murder, Basil ? You do say most startling things at times."

" But this isn't Kit's murder, is it ? " he said. " You don't think that, do you ? "

" Why, no, I don't think that had even occurred to me. For one thing . . ."

D

" Well? "

" D'you think Kit has ever heard of stuff called phenyl-thiourea? "

Basil seemed, for just an instant, to be a little surprised. He glanced round at her, his eyebrows raised. Then he looked back at the road ahead of them, which was not quite dark yet, but in that state of half-light when the headlights of a car only create a flicker of deceptive shadows.

" So you've worked that out, have you? " he said. " How did you manage that? "

" Laura worked it out," Clare said. " That's why I'm here."

" Ah yes, I thought she'd get round to it sooner or later. But I didn't think of her going to you with it."

" So you've known from the first? "

" I don't *know* even now," he said. " But it was obviously a possible explanation of Sir Peter's ability to eat that lobster. Someone who knew of that idiosyncrasy of his might have thought it was a safe way to kill him without harming anyone else."

" But Laura believes that it was she who was meant to be poisoned."

" Of course," he said. " She is—I think she always was— a rather self-important young woman."

A sudden sense of calm descended on Clare. She gave a sigh and muscles that without her realising it had been tense for hours, so that she ached from head to foot, relaxed and let her have a feeling of peace and comfort.

" I might have known you'd have it all in hand," she said.

" Ah, but I haven't," he said, " and I can't tell you how grateful I am for this visit of yours, because I haven't yet explained any of this to Fanny. It isn't the kind of thing she'll grasp very easily. I'm so afraid she'll simply transfer her certainty that she killed Sir Peter to an even greater certainty that she nearly killed Laura—and she may even persuade herself that she had an unconscious motive for doing this, so that she can't really plead accident any more. And her conscience has been giving us all a rather terrible time as it is."

" But you say she knew nothing about this bitter-tasting stuff? "

" Nothing at all."

" You told her there was something peculiar about Laura, but never what it was? "

" Yes. At first I didn't remember myself what it was, I just knew that the name, Laura Greenslade, meant something unusual to me, and forgetting what Fanny's imagination can do with an odd bit of information like that, I said as much. After that, when the facts about her suddenly came back to me, I felt that Fanny would think them such an anti-climax that I could hardly tell her. Science is fundamentally uninteresting to Fanny."

" But, Basil, that means. . . ."

" It means that if anyone tried to murder Laura, I did, doesn't it? "

" No," Clare said, " of course not. It means that Sir Peter must have been the right victim after all. Which is what I've thought myself all along, in spite of Laura's determination to draw attention to herself. But there's still another possibility and I'm not sure it isn't actually the likeliest of all, and that is that there was never any intention of murder. Someone wanted to spoil Fanny's party, that's all. Whoever it was never thought that one person would get all the arsenic."

" Did that detective-inspector suggest that to you? "

" He did, as a matter of fact."

Basil nodded. " And to me too. It's a nice theory, of course."

" Only you don't believe in it," Clare said after a moment.

" Only *he* didn't believe in it," Basil said.

After that they were both silent and a minute or two later Basil stopped the car in front of his house.

Fanny must have been listening for them, for she came to the door and opened it before they reached it. Her face had lengthened with anxiety and lost some of its colour. Her manner was both subdued and restless. She seemed eager to see them and yet at the same time hardly able to drag her thoughts out of some dreary dream of their own. She was wearing slacks and her grey knitted sweater and for once no jewellery of any kind. A cigarette dangled from her lip with half an inch of ash on it. As Clare came up the path she saw the ash drop and settle unnoticed on Fanny's bosom.

As usual Fanny spoke immediately about her own affairs.

" I've shut the shop," she told Clare. " Ever since Saturday we had such a stream of people coming in, I was disgusted. Don't you think it's disgusting? Could you ever do a thing like that yourself? Why are some people like that? "

Basil laughed and said, " And I told her that now at last she had a chance to make some money."

" You didn't, you were the one who advised me to shut it," Fanny said solemnly.

She turned and went back to the sitting-room, her slippers making a sliding sound as she shuffled them down the stone passage.

There was a big log fire burning on the hearth. The room was warm and cheerful, gay with bowls of spring flowers. Kit was sitting by the fire, reading an evening paper. He got to his feet as Clare entered and gave her an uncertain smile. He was showing the signs of strain even more than Fanny. Looking at Clare with an intensity of questioning in his blue eyes, he was wondering, she supposed, if she had seen Laura, or perhaps even knowing from Laura herself that she had done so, was trying to guess what had brought her.

She sat down close to the fire, thankful when Basil, remembering as usual her shrinking dislike of cats, picked up Martin, who was showing an eager interest in her ankles, and thrust him out into the passage.

After that Basil brought her sherry, while Fanny, taking the chair facing Clare across the hearth, picked up her own half-empty glass.

" Well," Fanny said, when she had gulped what was left in it, " what's happened? "

Clare wished that Kit was not in the room. That would have made it easier to talk. With his intent, anxious gaze upon her, she felt a great embarrassment at having to speak of Laura. Then, to her relief, Basil began to speak for her, and told Fanny and Kit of Laura's visit to Clare, of Laura's peculiarity, of Laura's suspicion, of the inspector's questioning and suggestions.

Kit turned away in the middle of it, sitting down, leaning back and fixing an expressionless stare on the ceiling. Fanny, frowning, fixed a steady gaze on his set face. She took the information that her future sister-in-law suspected her of having attempted to murder her with surprising calm, even, Clare thought, with a trace of relief.

Fanny's first words, when Basil stopped, were, " Well, at least that makes some sense of it all."

Kit exclaimed something unintelligible. It had the sound of bitter anger, but against whom the anger was directed was not clear. He did not move.

Fanny went on, " And I suppose really it's perfectly natural that Laura should suspect me. That's what I think I'd do in her place."

" However," Basil said, " I don't think *we* need waste time on suspecting you. The question is, how are the police going to like the theory that Laura, and not Sir Peter, was the poisoner's object? "

" They aren't going to like it much," Fanny said, " yet it could easily be true. *I* think it's probably true."

" With you as the poisoner? " Clare asked sharply, annoyed that Fanny should be ready to help Laura in her dramatisation of the relations between them.

" No," Fanny said.

She said no more just then, but Clare could see that some thought had started working in her mind, some thought that comforted her and gave her peace.

With a look of helplessness, Clare turned back to Basil. He shrugged and smiled.

At that moment Fanny abruptly stood up, went purposefully to the door and out into the passage, took her old coat from the peg on the wall, draped it round her shoulders and went quickly out of the house.

CHAPTER ELEVEN

SHE WALKED down the path and out into the quiet village street.

Darkness had come by now, broken only by the lights in windows, most of them closely curtained, and by the few street lamps under the elms. The sky was starless, covered in low cloud. It was cold, with a sharp wind blowing.

Fanny tightened her coat about her, but she did not hurry to keep warm. She was not going anywhere in particular. She had come out simply to give herself a chance to take a firm hold on a thought that had come to her while Clare had been speaking. If Kit had not been in the room she would not have come out at all. But Kit's presence had made it impossible to discuss her thought with Clare and Basil, and to have remained there with them, pretending to think about something else, would not have been possible to Fanny.

Walking along slowly, talking quietly to herself, she put her thought in order. It was an astonishingly reassuring thought, for it lifted the load of guilt from her shoulders. In a way, it did even more than this. It convinced her that her feelings, her intuitions were reliable. It put her back on terms with her own nature that she could understand. For the first time since hearing of the death of Sir Peter, she felt like herself.

Besides this, she felt suddenly at peace with her surroundings. Guilt had made her feel that this small, pleasant world of hers, which was extremely dear to her, had turned, had had the right to turn, against her. But this evening it was her friend once more, accepting her and supporting her.

Walking on to the point where the houses of the village ended, she hesitated there, then went on a little farther down a narrowing lane. She knew the way so well that she hardly noticed the darkness. The roughness of the ground under her feet and the shadowy pattern of the hedges against the sky were familiar. But the wind cut more keenly here and after a few minutes she turned back. She walked more rapidly now as the comforting remembrance came to her that after all there was someone with whom she could talk over her precious thought. She knew where to find him, too, at that hour. Walking on past the gate of her own home, she turned in at the doorway of The Waggoners.

There was perhaps just a moment of silence in the bar as she entered. It was the first time that she had come in there since the day of her disastrous party. But after that first moment she was greeted with the usual good evenings, and Colin Gregory, in his accustomed corner, asked her what she would have to drink. As she sat down beside him, he added, " Glad to see you coming out of mourning, Fanny. How are things? "

" Fine," she answered. " Just fine, Colin."

The sound of the slow, country voices in the room, the crackle of the big fire, the snug familiarity of it all, wrapped her round in reassurance and calm.

Colin looked at her thoughtfully.

" Something's happened," he said. " You really do look better."

She nodded and smiled. Sipping her drink, she felt that it was the first that she had actually enjoyed for days. " I didn't kill Sir Peter," she said.

" You fail to surprise me," Colin said. " No one but you ever thought you did."

" Oh, they did," she said. " They must have. They didn't think I'd done it on purpose, but they thought it was my fault. I could feel it."

He shook his head. " You just felt what you were thinking yourself. It's a good sign that you've changed your mind. What made it happen? "

" Simply finding out how Sir Peter really was killed," she answered.

" Simply that? "

" Don't laugh at me," she said. " I do know. I haven't decided what to do about it yet, but at least I know how it

was done and that it wasn't by my own muddling and
bungling. I know who did it too."

"Who, then?"

"Laura."

He went on looking at her steadily for a moment without
saying anything. It was a good-humoured look but sceptical.
It spurred her on, more than further questioning would have
done, to explain herself.

"She didn't mean to kill him," she said, "any more than
I did. I was the person she meant to get at. I don't mean
she meant to poison me, but she meant to hurt and humiliate
me. You see, she's tremendously jealous of me because of
Kit. She thinks I'm going to try and hold on to him. She
thinks I'm going to keep him here in this job I made for him
and make him go on living with Basil and me. I suppose
that's all my fault because I didn't make it clear to her when
she came here that I only wanted to help. If he can find some
other job and wants to go away, I'd naturally never dream
of interfering."

"And does he want to go away?" Colin asked.

Fanny stirred uneasily.

"I haven't asked him directly and I don't mean to," she
said.

"I see."

She gave him a doubtful glance, then went on, "Really,
Colin, I do know what I'm talking about. I've been thinking it
out very carefully. I went for a walk by myself just now and
thought it all out. You see, Laura has the peculiarity that
she can't taste some chemical or other with a name I can't
quite remember, but Basil can tell you all about it. And she
found out that she had this peculiarity when she was at the
university and volunteered as a guinea-pig in some experiment
of Basil's. The stuff's got a frightful bitter taste to most
people, but just a very few people can't taste it at all. Her
idea was to use it and a little arsenic to make my lobster taste
foul and give everyone tummyaches, getting out of it all
herself by having a phoney headache. But of course she
made several mistakes. To begin with, she didn't know how
much of the stuff to use. Not being able to taste it at all

herself, she probably thought she had to use a lot to be sure
that other people could, and so she put in so much that in
fact they could hardly swallow the stuff at all and so weren't
affected by the arsenic. And another mistake which she
couldn't have known about, was that there was another
person at the party who couldn't taste this stuff any more
than she could. I gather that's a very unlikely thing to
happen, yet it *can* happen. . . ." She paused, seeing that
look of reserve on Colin's face that she generally connected
with the idea of an unvoiced criticism. " You don't think
much of it," she said.

" My mind's quite open," he answered.

" I don't think it is," she said. " I think you think I'm
talking rubbish."

" It's just that it's all a bit complicated," he said. " It
would be so easy to make something taste a bit unpleasant
without using this mysterious substance you're talking about."

" Of course it would," Fanny said. " *And perhaps she didn't
use it.*"

He gave a slight shake of his head. " I don't get it, I'm
afraid."

Fanny herself had only just thought of the point she was
about to explain to him and she had to frown and purse her
lips in a great effort to clear her mind before she went on.

" Look," she said at length, " nobody knows that that
stuff was actually used. But Laura's going to go to the police
and tell them that it was—*that's* the whole point of the
thing. She'll tell them that and then tell them that Basil was
the only person who knew about this peculiarity of hers—or
—or perhaps she won't actually go to them and tell them
that, but she'll threaten to, to try and make us do whatever
she wants. Of course I don't know quite what's going on in
her horrid little mind, but you'll see, it'll be something of
that sort."

She thought that at last she had made an impression on
Colin. A frown appeared on his usually tranquil face and
his eyes searched hers for a moment, as if he were trying to
draw out of them something more than she had said. But
then he said, " Fanny dear, have another drink."

" What's wrong now? " she said. " What have I said now that doesn't make sense? "

" It's just that you've said a bit too much," he said. " Some of it might make sense without the rest of it."

" Such as which? "

" Well, spoiling your party and your reputation as a cook by giving everyone a little pinch of arsenic in the lobster is one thing," he said. " But faking up a case of attempted murder against you and Basil is another."

" Well then," Fanny said, " the one I'll stick to is the faking up a case of attempted murder against me and Basil."

" It's evident," he said, " that you don't really like the girl."

The statement moved her to a fit of nervous laughter. Beginning quietly, it suddenly seemed to take a twitching hold of her muscles, so that she felt herself shaking and chuckling without any true sense of amusement. She saw heads turning towards her and eyebrows curiously raised, yet she could not stop until Colin, taking a hold of her wrist, tightened his grip on it till it hurt.

" Listen," he said in her ear, " you've given me an idea and it isn't a nice one."

Though her laughter had stopped, Fanny was still breathless.

" You mean," she said, " that she could plot . . . that she could actually . . ."

" No," he said, " it's nothing to do with Laura."

" That's because you didn't meet her," she said. " The moment I saw her, I thought——"

" No," he said with some impatience, " don't you see that if the girl had really plotted anything of the sort, she'd never have had that headache you think was phoney. She'd have been careful to be one of the victims herself."

" Except that her courage might have failed her."

" But then her whole scheme would have collapsed, because she'd have had to convince the police that you and Basil, having plotted to kill her in this extraordinarily elaborate way, and finding that your victim wasn't even going to 'touch the poisoned lobster, could still have given the stuff to your other guests. That just won't do, you know."

" But . . ."

" No," he said, " come down to earth. Your first suggestion really opens up a lot more possibilities—that you were meant to be hurt and humiliated, and that's all."

Fanny gave a sigh. " The scheme worked then, didn't it? " she said. " The only trouble is—well, to be absolutely honest, I don't quite see what Laura had to gain by doing that. The other scheme would have had a sensible object in its way. I mean, it would have given her something to blackmail me with. But just humiliating me . . . After all, Kit wasn't likely to care for me less because I made a fool of myself at a party and cooked a rotten lobster."

" No, you're quite right," Colin said.

" Well then . . . ? "

He did not answer. An absent look had settled on his face and although his eyes were again looking into hers, Fanny felt that this time he was hardly even seeing her.

The look disturbed her because in the mood that she was in, anything that she did not understand seemed capable of holding some menace for her. She stood up.

" Anyway, thanks for listening," she said.

" Oh, I'm a great listener."

He stood up too and as she went to the door, followed her.

Out in the dark street, he went on, " I wonder if you'd listen now to a word of advice, Fanny. Don't tell these ideas of yours to everyone you meet."

" Why, what d'you take me for? " she said. Then after a moment she smiled. " Yes, I know, I do chatter, don't I? "

" Just a bit."

" And you think it might be libellous or something? "

He hesitated, then said cautiously, " Just possibly."

" All right," she said, " I won't tell anyone but Basil. But you haven't told me yet what your idea is, Colin."

" I haven't got it thought out," he answered.

They walked along together. The wind had grown stronger and the tops of the elms were stirring and the boughs creaking over their heads. As they reached Fanny's gate, Colin put a

hand on her shoulder and gave it an encouraging squeeze,
then went on to his own gate. As soon as he had separated
from her, the look of absence and uncertainty on his face
became one of hurried purpose. Going quickly up the path
to the house, he let himself in and went in search of Jean.

He found her in the small, bare room that she used as an
office. There was a pile of correspondence on the desk in
front of her. She was looking tired but when he came in, she
leant back in her chair, raised her face to him and smiled.

The smile vanished as soon as she saw his expression.

" What is it? " she asked.

" Jean," he said, " how dangerous a man is Tom Mordue? "
She merely looked blank at the question.

" Tom Mordue," he repeated impatiently, as if he had
expected her to know instantly what he was talking about.
" Is he simply a crank with a streak of spite in him, or is he
a really dangerous man? "

She frowned, trying to find the answer that he wanted.

" I've always thought he was just a rather unhappy sort of
crank," she said.

" So have I," Colin said grimly, " but I've just been
having a talk with Fanny and she's put a new and unpleasant
idea into my head."

" About Tom? "

" She didn't mean it to be about Tom. She was thinking
of Laura Greenslade. But if someone suggested to you that
Poulter's death was the more or less accidental result of a
piece of spite against Fanny, whom would you think of at
once as the most spiteful person you know? "

" But how could it have been—accidental? " Jean asked.

" If his death hadn't been intended. If no one's death had
been intended. If all that was meant to happen was that
Fanny's guests should get sick and think that she'd given
them some bad lobster."

" But that would mean . . ." She stopped and her tired
face looked drawn. " No," she said in a low voice, " no, you
don't think that seriously."

" It's a possibility, isn't it? "

" That Tom should put arsenic into the lobster as a sort

of revenge on the Lynams because of Kit's engagement and then calmly watch while one man ate the lot? "

" That's why I asked you, *is* Tom a really dangerous man? "

" A dangerous lunatic? "

" If you like," he said.

She started to say something, checked it and went on looking at him intently, while Colin returned the look, still with that touch of impatience, as if he were waiting for some response from her that she had failed to give.

After a moment she said reluctantly, " I suppose he could have got into the Lynams' kitchen without being seen."

" Easily," Colin said.

" And he was here that afternoon. If he'd gone straight round there when he left us . . ."

" Yes."

" And his state wasn't normal. But . . ." She was still trying to feel her way towards the answer that she could feel him demanding from her. " But the bitter taste, Colin. Why poison the food and then put in something to stop people eating it? "

" Suppose," he said, " someone else added the bitter taste —having followed Tom and slipped into the kitchen as soon as he left."

" But who? " she asked incredulously, yet with a feeling of horrified understanding.

" Minnie would go through anything to protect Tom," Colin said. " If she'd known what he meant to do and couldn't stop him—and she can never stop him doing anything he's set his mind on—what might she think of doing to protect Fanny and in a way Tom himself, which, if it had worked out as she intended, wouldn't have given him away to anyone? "

" But that would have meant that Minnie as well as Tom knew what Sir Peter was eating, and that's something I can't believe."

" Can't you? " Colin said. " The odd thing is, I can. I can believe it easily, because I think all Minnie's feelings are concentrated so completely on Tom that when she saw her scheme hadn't worked—in fact, by some horrible accident had made things much worse than if she hadn't interfered, actually turning Tom into a sort of murderer—she'd never have done anything to give him away. She'd have sat still like a fascinated rabbit, watching Poulter get all the poison. Come to think of it, what else could she have done?"

"The horrible accident," Jean said, "being Sir Peter's inability to taste whatever it was she used?"

"Yes. There are people who can't taste certain bitter things. I've just been hearing about it from Fanny, who's been told about it by Basil. And it happens that Laura is one of those people, so she's probably going to the police to tell them that Fanny and Basil tried to poison her, while Fanny's trying to make out a case that Laura faked the whole thing herself, just in order to be able to do that."

"And couldn't that—Fanny's idea, I mean—possibly be true?"

"I don't think so. I think if it were, Laura would have taken care to get some of the arsenic herself."

Jean nodded hesitantly, then turned away from him to look out of the window. To fit with the general bareness of the room, it was uncurtained and now, with the darkness beyond it, Jean could see herself clearly reflected in it, and, almost as clearly, Colin, as he stood, unusually tense and eager, near the door.

Addressing his reflection, she said, "You've been doing a lot of thinking about all this, haven't you?"

"Yes," he said in a rather flat tone.

"And I thought you were being extraordinarily indifferent to Fanny's troubles."

"For such a loving wife, you often get me wrong," he said.

"I do," she said. "It's true. What are you going to do now?"

"Do?" he said.

"I thought you looked somehow as if you were going to do something or other."

"What do you think I ought to do?" he asked.

"I don't know. Perhaps it would be a good idea to talk it all over with Basil."

He shook his head. " D'you know something? One never gets anywhere by talking things over with Basil. He's taken the art of helpfully saying nothing further than anyone else I know."

" Clare, then."

" She terrifies me."

" But you aren't just going to sit back now and do nothing! "

" You don't trust the police to do their own jobs? "

" Yes, I suppose I do. But all the same . . ."

He gave a laugh and at the sound of it Jean flushed and grew rigid. She said nothing and after a moment Colin went on, " You just want me to do *something*, don't you, whether it'll really be useful or not? Well, as a matter of fact, I was meaning to, though I'm not quite clear about its wisdom. If you'd suggested the same thing to me, I'd have felt a lot better about it."

His hand went out to the door.

Jean turned her head quickly.

" What are you going to do, Colin? "

" Go and see the Mordues."

" What, now? "

" Yes."

" Will that really do any good? "

" For all I know," he said as he went out, " it may do harm."

CHAPTER TWELVE

LETTING HIMSELF out of the house, Colin walked towards the garage which was at some distance from the house. Before he reached it, he changed his mind and decided to go on foot to the Mordues' cottage.

Though he did not hurry, for Colin hardly ever hurried, he did not notice the cold of the evening. Walking in the darkness was something that he always enjoyed. But usually, on an evening walk, he would have been alert for any twittering of birds in the trees or rustle in the undergrowth or the scents of the early spring, whereas to-night his mind was wholly occupied with his own thoughts.

The Mordues' cottage was a small, square box of Victorian brick. It was not old enough to be attractive but only old enough to have every form of inconvenience. It had an earth-closet, thirty yards from the house, down a path that for three-quarters of the year was either muddy or ice-covered. Its water supply was from a pump in a stone-flagged scullery. It had tiny, pseudo-gothic windows and there were rats in the wainscot.

Tom had always refused to spend anything at all on modernising the cottage. He claimed that as it was it had character and said that he had no intention of turning it into a suburban villa. Its garden, however, was relentlessly suburban, a rectangular lawn in front and weary-looking rows of brussels sprouts at the back. Its small rooms were neatly drab and overcrowded.

Minnie opened the door to Colin. When she saw him she looked scared.

" Oh! " she said in an astonished voice and went on looking at him with her mouth a little open, too startled to invite him in, too nervous to tell him to go away.

" Tom in? " he said cheerfully.

" Oh yes," she said.

From the sitting-room, Tom's shrill voice called out, " Who's there, Minnie? "

She was too petrified to answer.

Colin said softly, " Better let me tackle him, Minnie. He can't really go around avoiding me in a place like this. The strain's too great."

She looked more scared than ever. " But he'll never forgive you, Colin. And after all, interfering like that about Susan, —it wasn't right, you know."

" I meant well," he answered.

" But it was like criticising Tom," she said in a shocked voice.

" You know, I never thought of that," he said. " Believe it or not, I was just thinking about Susan."

" But you know what Tom's like."

" I do indeed."

" So don't you think it might be better now—? "

She could not bring herself to go on, so Colin finished her sentence for her. " If I just went away again? No, Minnie, I want to come in and talk to Tom. And you. And Susan, if she's here."

Again Tom called out, " Why the hell don't you answer, Minnie? Who's there? "

She made a weak gesture and stood aside. Colin gave her a reassuring smile and stepped into the little hall.

Tom was sitting close to a smoky fire in a small black iron grate. He sprang to his feet when he saw Colin, but he was taken too much by surprise to have any line of attack or defence prepared, and for a moment he simply stood there, holding his mouth tightly shut with the lips sucked in between his dentures, so that they were quite invisible.

During that moment Minnie plucked up her courage to say, " Now, Tom . . . Now just a minute, Tom . . . I think it's very nice of Colin to have called so that you and he can talk things over reasonably and I'll just go and make some tea. . . ."

Tom let his breath out with a little whistling sound.

" Talk things over—bloody nonsense! What have you come for? " he demanded.

Colin spoke deliberately. " There's been a certain amount of talk locally about a murder. I came to find out whether perhaps you mightn't have done it."

He heard a little gasp from a corner of the room. Turning his head, he saw Susan, who had been half-hidden by the high back of her chair. She stood up now, putting aside some sewing on which she had been working close to an old-fashioned paraffin lamp, the smell of which was strong in the small room. Her cheeks were warmly coloured from the heat of the lamp, but her eyes were cold.

" I'll make the tea," she said.

" Stay where you are," Tom said. " I told you, Gregory, and you should know by now I mean what I say, I znd my family want nothing further to do with you. I've always restrained myself with you before, on account of your wife, whom I very much respect, but since you took it on yourself to take unwarrantable liberties——"

" Cut it out, Tom," Colin interrupted. " You restrained yourself with me because I was one of the few people who troubled to restrain myself with you. And on a few occasions, that took all the restraint I had. To-night I'm going to say what I came to say and then I'll go away and I probably shan't come here again."

The speech startled them all. It was plain they had all assumed that Colin had come to see Tom in a spirit of conciliation. It was in character, so far as they knew his character, for him to do so. Tom Mordue looked oddly at a loss.

He muttered, " Well, since you're here, sit down."

" No, thank you," Colin said.

" Look, Gregory, " Tom said, " if I misunderstood you the other day and if you want to explain——"

" I don't," Colin said. " I haven't come to talk about that incident at all. I've come to talk about the death of Sir Peter Poulter."

" But what's that got to do with me? " Tom flung himself back into his chair and stared resentfully at Colin. His temper, stilled momentarily by the unexpected anger in Colin's voice, flared again. " If you've come here just to indulge a taste for sensationalism, you've come to the wrong place."

" I haven't," Colin said. " I've come to ask you what you had to do with it? "

" I? " The natural shrillness of Tom's voice thinned to an incredulous squeak.

Colin nodded.

" But—but—— " There was blank astonishment on Tom's face, but only for an instant. As he took in the fact that the words that he had heard had really been spoken, he turned with a look of agitated appeal to Minnie.

" What does he mean? " he asked shakily. " What can he mean? "

Minnie came forward to stand beside his chair, facing Colin.

"Yes, what do you mean?" she asked. Her voice was quite calm. She was afraid of very little on earth but Tom's displeasure, and the occasions when he showed his dependence on her, which were more frequent than the world knew, were the most inspiring moments of her life. "It isn't like you, Colin, to say silly things like that. Silly and nasty things."

Colin kept his eyes on Tom's face, though he replied to Minnie. "It isn't silly and I don't mean to be nasty, Minnie. I'm trying to act, believe it or not, like a friend. I'm trying to warn you, in fact. I had a certain idea this evening about what may have happened at Fanny's party and I think that sooner or later some other people may have the same idea. Wouldn't you prefer to hear about it from me, rather than —say, a detective-inspector?"

"But you're talking as if you thought we had something to be afraid of," Minnie said. Her voice was a little less firm than before and she moved still closer to Tom. "That's nonsense, of course. We were all terribly upset when we heard of Sir Peter's death and naturally we're all sorry beyond words for poor Fanny——"

"Just a moment, Mother," Susan said. "There's no point in arguing till we've heard what Colin wants to say." There was a sharpness in her tone which might have been meant to convey a warning to her parents. "Won't you tell us the rest of it, Colin?"

"Thank you, Susan," he said. "Yes—I don't want to drag this out. My idea was this. It's difficult to make sense of what happened at the party on the basis that a murder was intended. The method used was so slapdash that its chance of success was almost nil. Or so it appears to me. But suppose that something else was intended. Suppose somebody wanted to hurt and humiliate Fanny and in order to do that put a spoonful or two of arsenic into her famous lobster patties, so that all her guests would go home and be sick and say it was her fault. What about that? And then someone else, knowing that this had happened and deeply shocked at the idea, but also deeply attached to the person who'd put the arsenic into the lobster, thought the situation could be saved by adding something more that would make

the lobster uneatable, something—I don't know what—that
tastes violently bitter. And didn't know, of course, that Sir
Peter happened to be unable to taste bitter things."

" Stop! " Tom yelled. He had recovered his belligerence,
though his face was paler than usual. " I understand it all
now. This is how you're trying to pay me out for telling
you a few home-truths about yourself! A wonderful scheme!
And still trying to pose as my friend too! How many other
people have you whispered this story to already? It's round
the whole place by now, I expect, that Minnie and I between
us murdered Poulter."

" No, no," Minnie said hurriedly, " I'm sure that isn't so.
Colin would never think of spreading a story like that about
us. The truth is, he probably heard it from somebody else
and came here to warn us that it was going around. Of course
he knows it isn't true. For one thing, why on earth should
you want to hurt Fanny, of all people, Tom? She's your
best friend, the best friend of us all, in the village."

Tom managed to give a sour and scornful laugh. " Try
telling that to anyone and see if they believe you. No, this
is always what happens to people like me. We're always
made the scapegoats for other people's dishonesties and vices.
Because we don't flatter and cringe to them we're made to
pay and pay and pay! And when I only am involved, I don't
even stoop to defend myself, but when you try to drag Minnie
into it too——"

" Hush, dear," Minnie said, " we mustn't lose our heads
about this now, we really mustn't. Let's take it quietly and
think it all out sensibly. If we get too excited, Colin may even
think we've something to be afraid of. Now, Colin, tell me,
what *is* behind all this? I'm sure you don't really believe a
single word you've said. You do know what good friends we
are with the Lynams and that the last thing any of us would
do is try to hurt them."

For a moment Colin's gaze shifted from Tom's face to
Minnie's.

" I do believe that about you, Minnie," he said.

" You see, you see! " Tom cried. " A cheap revenge for
the straight talk I gave him the other day, that's the whole

explanation of this wonderful fabrication. And in a day or two it'll be round the whole place and the police will be coming here to ask us questions about it."

" I shan't take it to the police," Colin said, "unless I see Fanny or Basil or anyone else getting into serious trouble because of Poulter's death. Or unless anything else happens that seems to be maliciously directed against the Lynams. That's a fair warning, Tom, and I'd advise you not to forget it."

He turned on his heel and went out quickly.

He went out through the small hall into the dark garden, hurried along the path and out into the lane. There he paused for a moment as if he thought he might have forgotten something, then he started walking more slowly along the lane. The hard calm of his manner was unchanged, but a new thoughtfulness appeared on his face as he walked. It was an expression that not many people had seen, and after a moment, at the sound of quick footsteps behind him, it erased itself, leaving him with his usual air of good-humoured but rather lazy friendliness.

" Hallo, Susan," he said.

She came close to him, then stood still, peering into his face. She had on a loose overcoat and had tied a scarf over her hair. Her small, square face, in the darkness, was a pale blur.

" Why did you really do that, Colin? " she asked.

In a gentle tone, quite different from the one that he had used to her parents, he said, " Why d'you think, Susan? "

" I don't know," she said. " Why did you? "

" Perhaps because I think I've discovered the truth," he said.

She shook her head impatiently. " Of course it's not true, and you know it too—I'm almost certain you know it. For one thing . . ."

" Yes? "

She hesitated, then said, " Let's walk, it's cold."

They started walking again.

Susan at first seemed to want to walk rapidly, but in a moment her pace slowed down. Colin, strolling at her side, waited for her to go on.

" Actually I've been wanting to have a talk with you," she said, " about several things."

" The job? " he said.

" Yes, for one thing. I can't take it now, of course. It would look—it would look——"

" Why worry how it looks, if you want it."

" I'm not quite sure if I do want it—now," she said. " When you told me about it first I did want it, though not perhaps for the reason you thought. But now—I don't think I really want to go away any more. I hope that doesn't annoy you frightfully, after going to all that trouble on my account."

" It wasn't much trouble," he said.

" You see, I've begun to think I may have been wrong about something and if I was . . ." Her voice was full of embarrassment. " Colin, you thought I wanted to get away from Kit, didn't you? From Kit and Laura? "

" Well, yes."

" But really it was just my home I wanted to get away from, not Kit. It's funny, but everyone seems to have thought I was in love with Kit and that he jilted me. I don't know why they thought that. It isn't very complimentary to me, is it? " She gave a little artificial laugh. " The truth is, you see, it was the other way round. I jilted Kit. That's to say, when he asked me to marry him, I said no."

She stopped there as if she expected some comment, but Colin said nothing.

After a moment she said, " Don't you believe me? "

" Oh yes," he said.

" Well then . . .? "

" I was just wondering," he said, " why you refused him, and also how long ago it happened, and also why you're telling me about it now."

" I'm telling you about it because of that queer scene you made with Daddy this evening," she said promptly. " You haven't explained it to me yet, but I see you seem to think he's got a grudge against the Lynams on my account and I'm just showing you that that couldn't be so."

" Couldn't it? " Colin said.

She gave him a quick glance of anxiety. " What d'you mean ? "

" Just that—well, you've never told any of this to your parents, have you, Susan? There may be no real cause for Tom to have a grudge against any of the Lynams, but he doesn't know that, does he ? "

Susan stood still. Colin went on for a step or two, then realising that she was no longer beside him, paused and returned to her. She seemed to be gazing at him intently as he came towards her, but as soon as he looked into her face she turned it away from him.

" Of course he knows it," she said.

Colin said nothing.

" He does," she said more loudly. " And that—that's why, don't you see, he was so angry when you found that job for me and he thought I might want to take it. If he'd believed that I was unhappy because of Kit and that getting away from him would help me, he'd never have tried to stop me going. But he knew that he himself was the person I wanted to get away from. You see, in his heart, Daddy knows perfectly well how impossible he is and how people detest him and it frightens him horribly. And if ever he believed that Mummy or I had really turned against him, I believe he'd go out of his mind."

" I understand that," Colin said.

" I ought to have thought of that sooner, of course," she went on, " and not even played with the idea of going away. It was my fault really that you had that row with Daddy. I'm awfully sorry about it—and specially about all the trouble you've taken for me for nothing."

" It wasn't much trouble," Colin said a second time. There was a gleam of amusement in his eyes. " You're a quick thinker, Susan."

Her head jerked as she snatched a swift look into his face, then looked away again, staring woodenly into the darkness beyond him.

" You don't believe me, do you? " she said in a tired voice. " For some reason, you just don't want to."

" I believe you about Kit," Colin said. " But the trouble

there is that you've decided now that you are in love with
him, haven't you? "

One of her shoes made a scraping sound on the rough surface of the lane as she aimlessly moved her foot about.

" I'm not sure," she said.

" I'm fairly sure," Colin said.

" It's true, Laura was a shock," she said. " And at first I
was awfully angry about her, which may seem unreasonable
to you. I didn't even know she existed when Kit asked me
to marry him and then only a week later he was engaged
to her."

" I should have thought that was enough to make any girl
angry," Colin said. "But I find that I'm more than a little
sorry for Laura."

To this Susan made no answer.

He went on, " I wonder how much she knows of the
circumstances."

" I don't know what Kit's told her," Susan said. " Naturally
I haven't told her anything. But now that I've told you
such a lot about myself and my affairs, I think you ought to
tell me the real reason why you made that scene with Daddy
this evening—because it wasn't like you. You must have
known that walking in like that and hurling accusations at
him was the worst way possible of getting him to be reasonable."

" I wasn't, strictly speaking, trying to get him to be
reasonable," Colin said.

" Then what did you want? "

He cleared his throat, as if he were trying to think of an
evasive reply.

Before it came, Susan exclaimed, " You wanted—you
wanted to frighten *me!* Was that it? You wanted me to do
just what I've done and tell you all about myself and Kit! "

He shook his head. " But I did want to frighten Tom,"
he said. " You see, even if what I suggested isn't right, I
think he might know something about what really happened
at Fanny's party."

" He doesn't—I'm sure he doesn't."

" Then let's leave it at that, shall we? "

Again her voice became tired and discouraged. " I wish I understood more about it all," she said. " I keep getting a queer feeling that it's all my fault because I refused to marry Kit. But that doesn't make sense, does it? I refused him, you know, because of Fanny. I expect that's another surprise for you, because you know that I like her an awful lot. But the fact is that as long as she's around, Kit's never going to stand on his own feet, and besides, when I marry, I want a husband who'll really belong to me and not half to somebody else. And I told him all that."

" And so Laura was his answer, to prove to you his independence of Fanny," Colin said.

" D'you think so? "

He gave an abrupt laugh. There was a note of savagery in it.

" D'you know, Susan, I got you the offer of that job so that you shouldn't slip into the habit of hearing people say, ' Poor Susan.' I wonder what we shall have to do soon to stop them saying, ' Poor Laura.' "

She caught her breath sharply. Then without a word she started walking away towards her home.

Colin looked for a moment as if he might be about to follow her to say something more. But then he turned and went towards the village.

Presently he said aloud, " Poor Laura? "

He said it questioningly, experimentally, as if to discover whether or not it sounded appropriate and convincing.

A few minutes later, in much the same tone, he said, " Poor Susan ? . . . Poor Fanny? "

Then he laughed again.

CHAPTER THIRTEEN

COLIN DID NOT go home immediately. First he went to the Lynams'.

Fanny opened the door to him and was taking him, as a matter of course, to the sitting-room, from which the voices of Basil and Clare Forwood reached him, when he stopped her with a hand on her shoulder, saying, " Can I see you alone for a moment, Fanny? There's something I want to tell you."

" Let's go into the office, then."

She took him to the small room in which she and Basil had heard the news of Sir Peter's death from Dr. McLean.

Her face had lost the look of peace that it had worn when Colin had seen her earlier in the evening. Her theory, that had shifted the load of guilt from her own shoulders on to those of Laura Greenslade, appeared not to be wearing very well. But in the doubt and discouragement that made her shoulders sag and her plump cheeks look almost hollow, there was a new element of exasperation, of sheer bad temper, as if some pressure were developing in her that might shortly produce an explosion.

Throwing herself down in a chair and giving Colin an irritable, scowling stare, she said, "I've had nearly as much of all this as I can stand. D'you know what I'd do if I could? I'd pack up and clear out. Now. This evening."

" And not come back? " Colin asked.

" Not on your life! "

He answered with a laugh.

Snatching up a packet of cigarettes from the desk, Fanny fumbled inside it. The packet was empty and she flung it at the wastepaper basket, which it missed by a foot, falling on the carpet.

" Oh, what the hell! " she said. " It'll never be the same again, will it? "

" Why not? " Colin said. " This old village has seen far

worse things than an odd little case of poisoning and not been rocked to its foundations."

"Well, *I've* been rocked to *my* foundations," Fanny muttered. "I'll never be the same again."

"I'm sorry to hear that," he said. "I liked you as you were."

"You!" she said derisively. "You don't care about a single damn thing, so long as you've got your quiet life."

He had sat down on a corner of the desk and was giving her one of his steady but guarded looks, that gave away nothing of what he was thinking.

"I suppose that's very nearly true," he said after a moment.

Fanny stirred in her chair like a sulky child.

"Now for God's sake don't take anything I say personally," she said. "You should know better than that. It's just that this is all more than I can stand, it really is."

"I'd say that's a healthy sign," Colin said. "You were a little too anxious to carry the whole load yourself. All the same, what you said about me must be nearly true, because I'm quite surprised at how much I'm ready to do to protect this quiet life of mine. The fact is, I'm so well pleased with it, that I'm ready to go to considerable lengths to keep it just as it is—or as it was a week ago."

"What d'you mean?" Fanny asked. "What lengths are you going to?"

"Well, for one thing, I'm trying to put this lazy brain of mine to work," Colin said.

Fanny cocked her head on one side, looking at him frowningly and perhaps for the first time since he had arrived, giving him the whole of her attention.

"Yes," she said at length, "you're up to something or other."

"What I'm up to," he said, "is a sort of prevention-of-cruelty-to-Colin campaign, or, if you prefer it . . ." He paused and his tone changed, becoming entirely serious. "No, Fanny, there's no reason why I shouldn't be honest with you. The fact is that I can't bear the situation at the moment any more than you can. I've been sitting around seeing something that I value going to pieces—and I can't bear it. So I've got to do something about it."

"Something that you value . . ." Fanny said musingly. "Our sort of life here?"

"Of course."

"Yet we're all frauds, aren't we? None of us really belongs. The people who belong here are the farmers and the shop-keepers and some of the queer old maids who've lived here all their lives. People like us are just suburbanites who've put on country clothes." She glanced down discontentedly at her shapeless slacks. "And not even the right country clothes."

"What's that got to do with it?" Colin said. "We like it here. We like each other. And the village quietly goes its own way without taking much notice of us. In an over-crowded world, horribly tired of trying to make too many readjustments much too quickly, what could be more satis-factory?"

"You sound serious," Fanny said.

"I am serious," Colin said. "So much so, that to protect what I like, I'm developing an altogether new line of inter-fering in other people's business. And now I'll tell you why I came here. I've just been out to see the Mordues. I had an idea about them, put into my head by something you said, so I went out there to make an experiment. And the result of it was that I got told something that I'd half-suspected, though I wasn't sure of it. As a matter of fact, I'm not absolutely sure of it now. . . ."

He got off the desk and turned to the window. It was a small window with small panes, set high in the thick wall, and it faced towards his own home. One window there was lit up, the window of Jean's study.

Keeping his eyes on this light, he went on, "You see, Fanny, during the last few days I've kept getting the feeling that this whole thing must be my fault in some way. I know that doesn't make any obvious sense and I wasn't even taking it particularly seriously myself until this evening. I've had certain worries on my mind recently, among them the idea I'd had that I might be able to help Susan, and I thought

I was probably just mixing them all up together. . . . Well,
that part of it isn't important to anyone but me. But still, it
got tied up with an idea I had that there couldn't have been
any intention of killing Sir Peter. The method used was too
slapdash, I thought. It could have gone wrong so easily. As
a way of murdering anyone, it was chancy beyond words.
And then when you talked in the pub this evening about
Laura Greenslade having done it as a way of hurting and
humiliating you, I suddenly thought I saw something that
you hadn't. If anyone had wanted to do that to you, I thought,
it wouldn't have been Mrs. Greenslade, it would for certain
have been our dear old friend, Tom Mordue. . . ." He looked
round at Fanny. To his dismay, she was gazing vacantly at
the ceiling, with no sign on her face that she had been listening
to anything that he had said.

"Fanny——" he began.

"It's all right," she said. "Tom Mordue. Yes, I know.
The moment there's trouble of any kind, one's thoughts are
bound to fly to poor old Tom. I've been thinking of him
quite a lot, but I haven't said anything at all about it, because
he's the sort of dog everyone wants to give a bad name to
and hang. All the same, I don't think he'd have done anything
of that sort to me, I really don't."

"Don't you, Fanny? No, of course you don't." He
turned back to the window. "All the same, after my own
recent experience with him, I'm inclined to think that if
Tom were able to work out in that queer mind of his that
you'd done him an injury, there are almost no lengths to
which he wouldn't go to get even. And if Minnie knew of it,
there are no lengths, none at all, to which she wouldn't go
to protect him from the consequences of his own idiocy,
whilst doing her best to protect you—but still, Tom would
come first with her. And there you are—d'you see now what
my theory was, the one I thought of while we were talking
in the pub? I thought, Tom put the arsenic into your lobster
to make all your guests ill, then Minnie came along and put
some foul-tasting stuff in——"

"Phenylthiourea," Fanny interrupted. "I've got it
written down and learned it off."

"But we don't know that that's what it was, do we?" Colin said. "Let's just say something very unpleasant that was meant to stop people eating the lobster at all. And then it turned out that there was some defect in Sir Peter Poulter's sense of taste and so he ate up nearly all the lobster by himself. And Minnie couldn't, didn't dare stop him."

"No!" Fanny said. Her chair scraped on the floor as she jerked it back a few inches. "I don't believe a word of it."

"Nor do I any more," Colin said. "That is . . ." His voice was hesitant, as if there were something that he was keeping to himself, and Fanny's eyes, watching him now, filled with a new, uneasy doubt. He went on, "I've been out there this evening, trying shock tactics. I don't think they did much good. They scared Tom all right, but then in his heart he's permanently scared of the antagonism he rouses in people, so that by itself doesn't mean much. And Minnie rallied to him, of course, and so by now, if there's any fragment of truth in what I thought, they'll have a story of some sort concocted to defend themselves with."

"Let's hope to God they have!" Fanny said earnestly.

This time, as Colin looked round at her again, there was no smile on his face.

"It's murder," he said, with an unfamiliar edge on his voice.

"No, it isn't," she answered. "Not if it happened like that. They didn't mean to kill anyone and so it's manslaughter."

"Except," he said, "that they watched it happen and didn't prevent it."

"Oh God!" she said and thrust a frantic hand through her hair. "Well, it didn't happen like that, Colin!"

"No," he said, "probably it didn't. And, as I said, I don't think my visit this evening did much good, except that Susan followed me when I left and told me something about herself and Kit. Tell me, Fanny, isn't it your impression that Kit treated Susan rather badly, suddenly producing Laura when everyone thought he and Susan were going to get married?"

She nodded, though her forehead creased in a defensive

frown. She was resentful of any criticism of Kit but her own.

" Well, Susan's story," Colin said, " is that she'd refused to marry Kit before Laura appeared on the scene at all, which means, of course, that Tom, if he knew about it, had actually no grudge against you and no reason to put arsenic in the lobster."

" So that was it! " Fanny said. Her tired eyes brightened with interest. " Susan refused Kit! Aren't we all fools? "

" Well, that's what I want to ask you about," Colin said. " Did she? "

Fanny thought it over for a moment.

" You don't believe it, do you? " she said at length. " Why not? "

" I'm not sure that I don't believe it," he said. " In fact, I do believe it. The only thing is, I'm inclined to think the rejection wasn't meant to be permanent. I think she intended . . ." He paused. " Well, I may as well tell you, because I want very badly to know what you think about all this. I think she intended it as a way of putting pressure on Kit to move away from you. She told me that she was very fond of you, but that all the same she wanted a husband who was much more independent than Kit."

Fanny's eyes narrowed a little and her cheeks flushed a dull red.

" Susan said that—*Susan?* " she said.

" I'm afraid so—and I'm afraid, my dear, that any young woman is going to say it. I didn't drag that in just to hurt you, but because—well, because———"

" Because you wanted to tip me off? " she suggested bitterly.

" In a way. But mostly because I wanted to know, quite simply, whether or not you think that story's likely to be true."

Fanny's chair scraped again as she shifted it another few inches. Leaning back in it, she clasped her hands behind her head and her gaze went back to the ceiling, not vacantly this time, but with a calculating stare. The smoke from her cigarette drifted up towards a dark beam over her head and wreathed delicately around it.

"Well, it may be true," she said, "but I don't think it's true that Tom and Minnie knew anything about it. Minnie was horribly unhappy about Kit's engagement and didn't try to pretend not to be."

Colin nodded. "That's just about how I had it figured out."

"And if Minnie didn't know, Tom didn't. Susan might easily have confided in Minnie and not in Tom, and Minnie, just possibly, might have kept it to herself. But it could never have happened the other way round."

"Which means," Colin said, "as I thought, that Susan was frightened enough to lie about her parents."

"No," Fanny protested, "no, it can't. . . . That is . . . Well . . ." Her voice died away. The vacancy had returned to her face, making her look withdrawn from Colin, occupied again, as she had been ever since the death of Sir Peter Poulter, with uncommunicable thoughts of her own.

"Still, even if it were so," Colin said, "it doesn't neces- sarily mean anything, does it?"

Fanny did not answer.

"Or all it need mean," he added, "is that Susan was frightened for no reason at all, which can happen to the most sensible of us. And that brings me back, very reluctantly, I must say, to the possibility that after all somebody—some- body who knew you well enough to get into your kitchen and poison your lobster—did deliberately murder poor old Poulter."

"I don't think I'm reluctant to return to that idea," Fanny said, "not after the other things you've been sug- gesting."

"But it was such a messy, preposterous way of doing it," he said. "Ingenious at first sight, but really as stupid as hell."

"And none of us even knew Sir Peter——" She broke off the sentence abruptly. Colin seemed to take no notice of it, but from something in his face, she guessed that he was perfectly aware of what she had nearly said. It was always very difficult to Fanny not to say whatever was on her mind, and during the last few days she had had continuously on her mind the memory of Clare Forwood's uncharacteristic desire to meet Sir Peter. She coughed and said, "Of course, Laura says she knew him."

"Laura," he repeated after her. "Laura, the unknown quantity. Is she really as terrible as you seem to think her, Fanny?"

"Oh, for God's sake!" Fanny said. "I don't want to talk about her. She believes I tried to murder her, when in fact I was doing my best, my very best, to be nice to her. Now come and have a drink with the others."

"No," he said, "thanks. Jean knows I went to see the Mordues and she's probably anxious about the outcome. I'd better go home."

"You've told all this to Jean then?"

"Yes."

"And what did she think about it?"

"I hardly know."

Fanny heaved herself up from her chair, making such a labour of it that it was easy for a moment to see the old woman that she would one day become. "Well, thanks for coming, Colin," she said, "though I don't know what I'm thanking you for. You've only said a lot of things to worry me more than ever."

She went with him to the door. When he had gone she closed the door on him and stood there, her hand still on the latch, her face set in a frown of intense thoughtfulness. Then she returned to the sitting-room.

When she had left it Basil, Kit and Clare had been there together. Now only Kit was there. He was sprawled in a low armchair, holding open before him the local newspaper at the page on which sales of furniture were advertised. But Fanny knew as soon as she saw him that he was not reading the advertisements. He was only pretending not to be impatiently, nervously waiting for her return, to hear what she and Colin had been privately discussing.

"Where's Basil?" she asked.

"Gone to his room to work," Kit said. "And Clare's lying down or something."

Fanny sat down near the fire, fondling Martin the cat as he

moved closer to her to rub himself against her ankles. The sound of his sudden loud purring filled the quiet room.

It was scented with hyacinths, from a bowl that stood on the window-sill, beside the large, framed photograph of Laura. Fanny's face, as she sat down, looked stern and at the same time forlorn and rather bitter.

Minutes passed before either she or her brother spoke again. Then Kit, still holding the paper up before him, grunted, " What did Colin want? "

Fanny did not answer. She was leaning forward in her chair, as if she wanted to get as close to the warmth of the fire as she could.

Kit did not repeat the question but behind the screen of the newspaper his heavy jaw jutted forward and his lips moved for an instant. Then he tossed the paper aside, stood up and planted himself, still silent, with his back to the fire. His thick-set body, his ruddy face, his blue, bewildered eyes expressed an almost desperate protest.

Fanny was hardly aware of it. Her mind was full of her own desperation and her own protest. She remembered the peace that she had felt for a short time earlier in the evening when it had seemed apparent to her that the burden of guilt which, against the arguments of everyone else, she had insisted on taking up, could be justifiably shifted on to the shoulders of Laura Greenslade. Colin had destroyed that peace, first by his refusal to be impressed by her argument and later by hinting at new and unspeakably disturbing possibilities in the situation. She felt now a muddled and distracted anger against him because of it, yet she did not doubt for a moment that his insight was clearer than hers.

Once or twice, staring at the fire while Kit stood tensely near her, she sighed sharply and impatiently. Her hand, without her being aware any longer that it was doing so, went on stroking the relaxed and contented body of the cat.

When at last she began to speak, it sounded as if she were taking up an argument in the middle. She spoke in a low, puzzled voice.

" What I don't understand is why anyone should have

ideas like that about me—that I'm possessive, that I'm jealous, that every time I try to do something reasonably helpful I'm simply doing it so that I can keep a tight hold of you. I don't understand—that's to say, I do, I do understand it perfectly in Laura, but to find that Susan—Susan of all people——"

" What about Susan? " Kit said quickly.

" She hates me," Fanny said.

" What rot! " Kit said.

" No, she hates me so much that she wouldn't face becoming my sister-in-law—isn't that the truth? Isn't it, Kit? " For the first time she seemed to be speaking to him directly.

His face reddened, but he spoke more quietly than before. " No, not exactly. In fact, not at all."

" But you did ask her to marry you, didn't you, and she refused because of me? "

" I asked her to marry me and she refused me.".

" Because of me? " Fanny insisted.

" No," Kit said, " because she hadn't any use for me. That's quite a normal reason, isn't it? It doesn't need explaining."

" Only it isn't true—she's in love with you," Fanny said.

" Rot! " Kit said again, the red in his face deepening.

" And you," Fanny went on, " you were in love with her all the time, as I used to think you were, and you just went and got engaged to Laura to get even with Susan, of all suicidally imbecile things to do! And it's all my fault—that's what I discover—all my fault for being so possessive and jealous."

" Will you shut up! " Kit said fiercely. " I got engaged to Laura because I'd fallen in love with her and she with me. And Susan isn't in love with me and never has been. I ought to know that better than anyone, oughtn't I? "

" You ought, but you don't," Fanny said,

" I do," Kit said, " and if other people would realise that and leave me alone—and leave Susan alone—and Laura, we'd be able to sort things out without any difficulty."

" Even with Laura accusing me to Clare, and probably to the police by now, of having tried to murder her? "

"Well, what have you been accusing her of in your own mind?" Kit asked.

"I've only been doing my very best to help her and you, but it turns out that means I'm jealous and possessive——"

"God!" Kit shouted. "What the hell has that man Colin been saying to you? Have I ever said you were either, or been anything but damned grateful for all you've done for me, or shown any signs of wanting to walk out on you?"

"But that's what you ought to have done, it seems," Fanny said. "If you'd been ready to walk out on me, Susan would have married you, and then you'd never have got tangled up with that shallow, frightened, spiteful creature in London—and then probably none of these awful things would have happened. Why, oh why, *didn't* you walk out on me?"

Kit strode a step closer to her. "Is that what you want? I'll walk out on you now, this minute, if that's what you want."

"Don't be ridiculous."

"But it is what you want. You're beginning to hate me because of Laura. You've shown it ever since I told you about my engagement."

"I haven't. I'm not. I've only got near hating Laura since I heard she was trying to show that I'd tried to murder her."

"You've only got Clare's word for that."

"I trust Clare absolutely!"

"I'd sooner wait till I've heard Laura's side of it," Kit said. "When she comes to-morrow, I shall ask her——"

"To-morrow?" Fanny cried shrilly. "The inquest isn't till the day after."

"We happen to want to spend a little time together."

"And you mean I've got to put her up here, while she's actually going about saying I tried to poison her?"

"Not on your life! I've got her a room at The Waggoners."

"So she *won't* come here! She thinks I might be more successful this time, is that it?"

Turning away, going towards the door, Kit said, "You can put it like that if you want to."

Fanny's eyes suddenly filled with tears. "And you—you say you're in love with a woman like that. It isn't possible."

" That almost sounds," Kit said, with a new note of deliberate cruelty in his voice, " as if you've never been really in love yourself. But you'd better get used to the idea that I am in love with Laura—and that that means I'm going to stand by her."

" In that case—in that case——" By still staring at the fire, Fanny could conceal the tears in her eyes from Kit, but she did not quite succeed in keeping them out of her voice. " In that case, perhaps you had better move out—as soon as you can conveniently do so. And you'd better stay away until Laura's ready to come here and to eat and drink whatever I choose to offer her."

" All right," Kit said. " All right, if that's the way you want it. I'll go at once."

" Don't be silly. In the morning——"

" I'll go at once."

" Kit! "

But he was already through the door and striding along the passage. He went straight out of the house, slamming the door behind him.

Fanny sat still, the tears pouring steadily down her cheeks and her stout body beginning to tremble. For some minutes she told herself that he would soon be back, that he had taken no clothes with him, that he had probably very little money on him, that he had not even taken his overcoat.

But even while she told herself this, she knew that there was no point in sitting there, waiting for the sound of his returning footsteps.

CHAPTER FOURTEEN

BLINDLY, instinctively, Kit made for The Waggoners.

He was in a rage and Kit, in a rage, which was a condition in which he found himself far more often than most people realised, was inclined to drink heavily. The drink always seemed to dissipate the rage itself, let him enjoy an hour or two of excitable cordiality towards the world around him and had next to no physical after-effects. Its psychic after-effects appeared in a sullen and long-lasting depression, but though Kit knew, even while he was drinking, that this was unavoidable, and had a deep fear of this state of mind in himself, he always awaited it with an inner bravado, a silent fury with himself in which he dared the terrors of his own spirit to attack him.

It was not any thought of this that made him, this evening, stop sharply in the doorway of The Waggoners, turn and walk quickly away. It was simply that he realised, as he was about to enter the room, that would be full of familiar faces, that to-night of all nights he must do his drinking amongst people who did not know him too well. Something had happened to him which he had not begun to understand and he needed badly the privacy which the company of strangers would give him while he tried to come to terms with it.

The trouble was that by the time he had gone to the garage where he kept his small and delapidated car, had got it out, found that he was almost out of petrol, stopped at a pump to fill up and then had driven the few miles to the nearby small town, the town in which he was to meet Laura at the station next morning, it was almost closing time.

Going to the Station Hotel, he had a hurried and unsatisfactory drink in the small, bleak bar, then took a room there for the night.

His rage grew all the more intense for the frustration. He hardly slept at all, which was a new experience for him and one which he found curiously terrifying. He could hardly bring himself to believe that any emotions of his were capable of having such a dire effect on his generally healthy constitution. It was like feeling the onset of symptoms of an unknown disease, which, because of his ignorance of it, it was easy to believe must be fatal.

By degrees his sheer astonishment and fear at being unable to sleep filled his mind so completely that he even forgot his rage, forgot what had brought him there to the small drab room and the uncomfortable bed, forgot that he was homeless and jobless. Through this phase of restless dread, he passed on into one of weary apathy, which remained with him for what was left of the night and when he got up the next morning, drank watery tea and ate a discouraging sausage and presently went to the station to meet Laura.

She noticed his state as soon as she saw him. He did not look tired or pale and yet in some way looked dimmed and faded. This irritated her, for Kit's fresh good looks were of the greatest importance to her. The firm, healthy look of his skin, the brightness of his fair hair, his heavy, muscular look of vigour, were what provided him with his power over her. They were what convinced her that she loved him and wanted him, even though she recognised that as a human being he was rather more complicated than she thought really desirable.

He was excessively reserved, she had discovered, had moods and a streak of acute suspiciousness in his nature. But at least, as a rule, none of these qualities obtruded themselves much on her attention or was likely to be noticed by those whose opinion of him was valued by her. So long as he kept his air of youthful, blond, male energy, he was intensely attractive to her.

But she had no emotions prepared to cope with a Kit in whom the pulse of life seemed to have slowed. It made her feel uneasy and unsure of herself.

" What's the matter? " she asked him at once, as they walked side by side along the platform. " What is it, Kit? What's happened? "

" Nothing much," he said.

" But I can see that something has happened," she said. " Is it something more about this frightful business, this poisoning? "

" No, nothing's happened—nothing special," he said. It felt very important to him to make as little as possible of his break with Fanny, particularly in talking to Laura. " Of course, the whole situation's been getting us all down," he added, as if to admit this were a great concession.

" Of course," Laura agreed, but not with sympathy. Her tone was suddenly and cruelly sarcastic.

Kit's eyelids twitched. Reaching his car, putting her suitcase on to the back seat, he said, " I've got you a room at The

Waggoners. I hope it'll be all right. It's not exactly luxurious."

" It.doesn't matter," she said. She was thinking now of the fact that Kit had not kissed her or even touched her, and that his whole attitude, the slouch of his heavy shoulders which were usually held straight, the slight droop of his head and the way that his eyes avoided hers, meant for certain that she had trouble on her hands.

She had been prepared for this, realising that although the day before, on the telephone, he had taken quietly her announcement that she would not stay again in the Lynams' house and that he must find a room for her in the village, explanations and argument would be necessary when they met. But she had thought of having to give these explanations in an atmosphere of excited emotion and not in this curiously deadened, enervated air.

While the drive lasted, she and Kit hardly spoke to one another. Laura made use of the time to prepare the line that she meant to take with him. Taking a cigarette from her case without offering one to Kit and lighting it herself, she sat with her head turned away from him, looking out of the car window, as if she were wholly occupied in watching the new, pale shimmer of green on the hawthorn hedges.

There was no sign in her to-day of the panic and hysteria that she had revealed in her interview with Clare Forwood. She was as well groomed as usual, her dark hair sleek, her make-up delicate and careful. Her uneasiness and her thoughtfulness showed only in the rigidity of her rather expressionless face, and presently, when she stubbed out her cigarette, in the flash of savagery that went into the gesture.

Kit, without commenting on it, saw this and his eyelids twitched again.

The room that he had booked for her at The Waggoners was, as he had said, not luxurious. It was at the top of a narrow, steep staircase, which led up from The Waggoners' side entrance, which opened out of a small courtyard, where dust-bins stood. There was a brass bedstead in the room, a marble-topped washstand with a basin and jug upon it, a dressing-table set in front of the window, and shiny oilcloth on the floor. Laura looked pointedly at the small black iron grate, in which a carefully arranged fan of white paper implied that the landlady had no intention of lighting a fire.

In a falsely gentle tone, she remarked, " Well, it's clean."

Kit shrugged and said, " Sorry, the best I could do."

" Oh, of course," she said, still smoothly and gently, " I didn't expect anything better."

Sitting down on the edge of the bed, she drew her fur jacket closely around her, then lit another cigarette.

" I suppose you want me to explain what I said on the telephone yesterday," she said.

Kit had grasped the brass rail at the foot of the bed with both hands.

" Not particularly," he said. " Clare Forwood came down in the evening. I heard the whole thing from her."

" Ah yes, Clare Forwood. . . . I'm sorry now that I went to her." As Laura changed her position slightly the wire mattress sang under her. " I suppose you're furious with me. You don't see my point of view at all."

" As it happens," Kit said, " I see it perfectly, and in case you're interested, I moved out on Fanny and Basil last night."

Something gleamed in Laura's eyes, perhaps satisfaction, perhaps simply astonishment. Whichever it was, it was quickly, and with determination, extinguished.

" So then you agree with me," she said in a level tone.

" I do not," Kit said.

" I'm afraid I don't understand, then."

" I do not think Fanny's a murderess."

" I wonder," she said musingly, " what the law is on the point. If you attempt to murder one person but accidentally kill someone else instead, is that only manslaughter? I don't really think so."

Kit's grip on the brass rail was making the bed rock.

" I'm trying to tell you," he said in the hectoring tone that comes easily to anyone unused to explaining difficult thoughts, " I see your point of view although I think you're wrong. I know Fanny didn't try to kill you. But because of this queer kink of yours, not being able to taste this phenylwhatsit, I mean, just because of a silly sort of coincidence like that, I understand your being afraid that she tried to. But you're wrong."

" In that case, why did you move out? " Laura asked.

" Because Fanny was being damned stupid too and it got on my nerves."

", If you think I'm stupid . . ."

" Besides, I'm engaged to you. I naturally stood up for you."

" I'm glad to hear it," she said remotely. " I—I didn't feel sure that you would."

Kit reddened. " But there's something I've got to make you see before you do any more damage——"

" Damage? " she cut in.

" Like going to Clare Forwood with a story like that against Fanny. And like going to the police with it. *Have* you been to the police with it? "

She drew at her cigarette before she answered, puffed out the smoke and said quietly, " No."

" Well, don't go, then. Because if you do, I'll have to move in again with Fanny and Basil and—and I don't believe that you want that, do you? "

" But why should you have to do that? "

" Can't you see how it would look? You accuse my sister of murder and I choose just that time to leave her. It'd be quite impossible."

" But if I'm right? "

" You aren't, I've told you."

Laura stood up and began to move about the cold, clean, depressing room, looking for an ash-tray. Failing to find one, she tipped her ash into a pink and white china hair-tidy on the dressing-table.

" And suppose I don't go to the police? " she said.

" I—I should be grateful," Kit said.

" And not go back? "

" No."

" And come with me to London? "

" Well, as soon—as soon as I could."

" You mean, after the inquest."

" No, I mean as soon as I'm sure Fanny can get on without me."

Laura flung both hands out in a gesture of extreme impatience. " I simply don't understand you," she said. " You tell me you've made up your mind to leave her, but then you say you're going to go on hanging around until you're certain she can get on without you. At that rate, don't you realise, you'll never be able to leave. She'll see that you don't."

" No—you don't understand," Kit said. " For one thing, it was Fanny who told me to get out last night. I don't think I told you that."

" I don't think you did. But I don't think either that it makes the least difference, because I'm sure she never believed for a moment that you'd go. Though, as a matter of fact, it does mean that you're even more free to leave her than I thought."

" It doesn't, it doesn't mean a thing," Kit said, " because I don't think she knew what she was saying. And the point is, I've been doing a job for her. I've been running that antique show of hers and if I leave suddenly she'll simply have to close down."

" Well, why not? She and Basil don't need the money."

" No, but she does need something—something that's her own, to interest her. You didn't know her in the old days when she was on the stage and before she got it into her head that she'd got to turn countrified and domesticated. In other words, before she married Basil. She was—she was so awfully different then. She was slim and full of life and always doing something. But now, if she hadn't got her antique business, she'd do nothing at all and simply go to pieces. I know she would. And it'd be my fault and I couldn't stand that. So I've got to stick around—I really have, Laura—until she's got things sorted out somehow and found somebody to take my place."

" Which she'll be careful not to do! "

" She will when she understands that I mean what I say."

" When, when! " Laura said with an angry laugh. " So

all this time that you've been clinging to Fanny, you've managed to convince yourself that it was the other way round and that she couldn't get on without you. You know, you begin to remind me of my husband, Charles. He had a mother. Such a sweet old dear—oh yes—there was nothing she wouldn't have done for him. But she'd eaten him alive. I did my best to cut him free of her and put a little energy and ambition into him—I can't bear a man without ambition —but all he really wanted was to sit around with her, being told how wonderful he was and how little I appreciated him. And all the time he used to tell me how lonely she was and how she'd break to pieces if he didn't look after her. It was quite ludicrous. And it was the thing that killed him, because if he hadn't insisted on spending one of his leaves with her instead of with me and the baby, he wouldn't have been in the house with her when it was bombed."

Kit had watched her while she was speaking with growing surprise.

"But I always thought," he said, "you always let me think, that you'd been awfully in love with him. But you weren't. You hated him."

"I didn't, I was in love with him!" she cried. "I'd have come to hate him if he hadn't died, but I loved him at first. He was very good-looking and very clever and I knew he could easily become someone who amounted to something— that is, I believed he had the gifts for it. We were both very young, of course, much too young to have married, but I had tremendous faith in him. That was before I knew his mother. Later I——"

"Laura!" Kit said loudly, breaking in harshly on her flow of words. "I'm never going to amount to anything. You know that, don't you?"

She gave him a bewildered look, as if the interruption had made her lose the thread of her thoughts. But then her face softened suddenly. She moved towards him.

"We'll see about that," she said. "I don't think you've begun to know yourself yet, my dear."

"I know myself pretty well," he answered. "I haven't got gifts of any kind. I'm not ambitious."

" Wait and see," she said. " Wait and see what happens to you when you've got away from Fanny."

" No," he said, " that won't change. I'll work and I'll make enough for us to live on, but that's all you can expect."

" Aren't you leaving me out of account? There are a great many things I can do for you. I'm not so young and ignorant as I was when I married Charles. I've got quite a lot of influence in certain places. I know lots of people."

" Like Sir Peter Poulter."

Her body stiffened. For an instant her eyes looked glazed with fury. Yet Kit had said the words almost casually and as if he had no sense of saying anything with outrageous implications.

In the same tone he went on, " People like that aren't going to have any use for me, Laura. I'll try to do anything you want, that's to say, as soon as things are straightened out here I'll go to London with you and find myself a job there —provided, of course, that you don't go to the police with your crazy idea about Fanny—but you've got to understand it's no good expecting anything much of me. Do you understand that? "

She stood there as if she were thinking over carefully what he had been saying. Then she reached out her arms and slid them round his neck.

" Kit," she said with her face close to his, " Kit darling, aren't we being fools? "

" But you do understand——? "

" Of course I understand. And we're being fools, because we're almost quarrelling, just at a time when we should be helping each other most. Let's stop it and be nice to each other."

He gave her a light kiss on the cheek, then drew away from her.

" All right, what would you like to do? " he asked.

For a moment she looked put out, but then said briskly, " Let's go for a walk. It's a lovely morning. But first would you go and find the landlady and tell her that I've simply got to have a fire here. I'll unpack a few things and change my shoes while you're gone."

" All right," Kit said again, looking relieved.

He went out and went looking for Mrs. Toles, the landlady.

She was serving the first few customers in the bar and it seemed to Kit, as he came in, that she and the others there were all of them talking as fast as they could, and all at the same time, but that on his appearance there was a sudden silence. Then they all began to talk again excitedly and with an air of congratulation about them, while somebody gave Kit a slap on the back.

Mrs. Toles' voice, used to authority in her own bar, carried above the rest.

" So they've got them, Mr. Raven. Now we can all rest easy, and I must say, for your sister's sake and Mr. Lynam's too, we're all right glad. You'll tell them that from me, won't you? They must have been suffering something terrible, poor souls, worrying their hearts out over what could have happened. That's what I'd have done if I thought that someone had got something to eat or drink here in my hotel that wasn't right and made them sick, let alone them dying of it. But now they don't have to worry about it no more and we were all saying, just as you came in, how glad we are to hear it."

Kit looked from one face to another. Heads were nodded at him and broad, ruddy faces smiled.

" That's right," Fred Davin, the ironmonger, said. He had left his shop to look after itself even earlier than usual, and come in, apparently to celebrate.

" You mean they've arrested someone for Poulter's death? " Kit said.

" That's right," several people said at once.

Mrs. Toles went on, " It's those two who looked after him, poor old soul. They knew they'd got something coming to them in his will and of course they hoped they could put the blame on Mr. and Mrs. Lynam. And I must say, it's what I thought all along. I said so, didn't I, Mr. Davin? They aren't local people, that's what I said. What do any of us know about them, I said. You wait and see, that's who they'll be arresting. I said that, didn't I? "

Fred Davin nodded. " They found the arsenic in the

gardening shed, you see. Spilled on the floor, careless like.
I reckon they never knew it was there."

" But what about the phenylthiourea? " Kit asked.

" The what? "

Kit coloured. " Nothing," he said. " Just something—an
idea someone had. It doesn't mean anything now. I wasn't
thinking." He was almost incoherent and if anyone had
looked at his big strong hands, hanging at his sides, he would
have seen that they were trembling.

Forgetting all about asking Mrs. Toles for a fire for Laura's
room, Kit turned on his heel and went running upstairs.

The words that had been ready to pour out of him when
he saw Laura were cut off by the sight of her face. She was
standing by the window, holding aside the lace curtain and
peering out. There was a look of intense excitement about
her. Her eyes were glittering and her mouth was twisted in
a strange, tight-lipped smile.

" Come here quick! " she exclaimed. " Quick—tell me,
who's that, Kit? "

He came to her side and looked out of the window.

In the street below, walking along with a shopping basket
on one arm, was a slim bareheaded figure, wearing a loose
grey coat buttoned high to the neck and somehow suggesting,
by its severity or else because of something in the personality
of the wearer, the habit of a nun.

" There was a man with her just now, but he went into
the tobacconist's," Laura went on. " Who is she, Kit? Do
you know her? "

" It's Jean Gregory," Kit said. " Why? "

" Jean Gregory? " Laura said.

" Mrs. Gregory. She lives next door to us. Why, have you
seen her before? "

Laura began to laugh. She laughed with a wild, excited
gaiety. " Mrs. Gregory, the awfully rich woman who lives
next door to you? " she cried. " She's rich, isn't she? She's
rich! "

" I suppose so," Kit said, uncomfortable and bewildered.
" Reasonably well off, anyway." As Laura broke into more

laughter, he repeated with a pang of anxiety, " Why, Laura?
What's got into you? "

" Nothing," she said. " Nothing whatever. Let's go for
a walk."

CHAPTER FIFTEEN

IT WAS AT about five-thirty that afternoon that Fanny, who
in a half-conscious way had not yet given up listening for
Kit's footsteps, heard them on the path and then in the
stone-flagged passage.

Outside the door of the sitting-room they stopped. Fanny
made no movement. It was possible, she knew, that Kit had
returned merely to fetch some of his belongings from his
room and that he did not want to see her. If that should be
so, she was determined to give no sign to anyone that she
had the slightest desire to see him.

Since she could not see her own face, she believed, during
the long moment when the footsteps went no farther in any
direction, that she was carrying out this decision successfully.
All her powers were concentrated on listening for them to
continue, so she did not notice that conversation in the
room had ceased and that all the people in it were looking
at her.

Basil, Clare and Colin were there. They had just finished
having tea and had been talking in a mood of subdued
satisfaction, of the arrest of Sir Peter's servants. To have
been satisfied in anything but a rather subdued fashion would
not have seemed decent, but it had been impossible not to
show some relief at the lifting of the cloud.

Nevertheless, it had not only been a sense of propriety that
had made their expression of this relief very moderate. Fanny
herself had had only half her mind upon it. She had been
thinking far more of Kit than of the murder. At the same
time Colin had not seemed to be really much impressed by
the news of the arrest. Either the whole subject had begun to
bore him or he was keeping most of his thoughts concerning
it to himself.

At last the door opened and Kit came in. He looked tired, self-conscious and not quite certain what he was doing there.

" You've heard the news, I suppose," he muttered.

Fanny nodded briefly and asked, " Where have you been? "

" To the pictures," Kit said.

" The *pictures?* All day and all night? "

" No, this afternoon. I spent the night at the Station Hotel." The horror of that night came into his voice as he said it.

" And where's Laura? " Fanny asked. " The fact that two people have been arrested for the murder of the Poulter man hasn't convinced her that I didn't try to poison her? "

" She's resting," Kit said defensively.

" You look as if that's what you ought to be doing," Fanny said.

" I'm all right." He came forward into the room and dropped into a chair.

Basil got to his feet. " You could do with a drink," he stated.

" Just a minute," Fanny said. " Kit, I want to know, what are you going to do? Have you come here to stay, or to talk things over or just to collect your things? "

Before Kit could answer, Colin stood up.

" I think I'll be going," he said.

" Why not stay and have a drink too? " Basil said.

Colin shook his head with a smile and went to the door.

" See you later," he said, and went out.

Fanny wished that Clare also would have the tact to absent herself for a little while, but she did not move. She was sitting close to the fire, looking drained of all energy, and rather as if she were hoping that the others there would get up and go out and leave her to recover a little from the terrible pressure of human contact.

" Well? " Fanny said to Kit when the door had closed on Colin.

" I came to talk about things," he said. " I wanted to tell you that as soon as all this has blown over, I'll be going to London. That's what Laura wants. I've promised her I'll do it."

" Why not go at once then? " Fanny asked frigidly.

" Well, I thought I'd wait till—well, anyway till you've got someone to do my job," Kit said.

" Thanks," Fanny said. " But that isn't important. I've been thinking recently I'd close the shop as soon as you'd found some other job for yourself."

" What Kit means," Basil said gently as he poured whisky into a glass, " is that he doesn't want to leave so long as his doing so could be mistaken for support of Laura's accusation that you tried to poison her. By the way, Kit, has she offered her theory to the police yet? "

" No," Kit said, " and she isn't going to."

" I should hope not," Fanny said, " now that the murderers have been arrested."

Basil brought the glass to Kit, who reached for it gratefully.

" Those were her terms, were they, Kit? " Basil said. " She keeps her mouth shut and you go to London? "

Kit swallowed some whisky and did not answer.

" Well, don't worry," Basil said. " It's probably the best thing for you to do anyway."

" It's all just as I thought," Fanny said with intense bitterness. " She never believed her own accusations at all. They were just a dodge for putting pressure on Kit. If there'd been anything genuine about them, she'd be round here now apologising to us for her preposterous suspicions, instead of *resting*. Is she going to come and apologise, Kit, or is she going to go on trying to remain the central character in the drama? "

Kit scowled ferociously at the fire.

" She says—she says that the bitter taste of the lobster hasn't been explained," he said.

In a dry, exhausted voice, Clare said, " As it hasn't, you know."

Turning to Basil, Fanny said peremptorily, " I want a drink too."

Clare went on, " One supposes the police think they can explain it and perhaps they'll tell us all about it soon. On the other hand . . ."

" I know," Basil said. " All those coincidences are worrying you, aren't they? Two people in one room who can't taste phenylthiourea, and at least one person there who knew that fact about one of those people—and some lobster that tastes bitter. . . . That makes the arsenic itself seem almost irrelevant, and as for these two poor people who've been arrested, they hardly seem to belong in the case at all."

" Well, coincidences do happen," Clare said. " That detective himself warned me to remember that."

" Of course they do," Fanny said. " They happen all the time. Look at the way one's always meeting people one knows in the most unlikely places. I hardly ever go to London for the day without running into someone I know. And there's nothing really difficult to explain about the bitter taste. It was just something the matter with my cooking. I've been saying that all along. It isn't at all unusual, even at the best of times, for something I cook to taste completely different from how I intend, and that day I was particularly nervous and muddled. But with the arsenic it was different. I don't keep arsenic in the kitchen cupboard."

" So we can all rest in peace," Basil said. " I hope Laura will come round to that view of the matter soon."

Kit looked as if he were trying to smile in response to this.

" Of course she will," he said without conviction.

Fanny took this dubious reply as an attempt at conciliation and at once was filled with eagerness to respond to it. " Listen," she said, " I've got an idea. Laura was awfully impressed by Clare, wasn't she? Well, I think Clare should go and see her now. I think, now that those people have been arrested, Clare might be able to get her to see reason. And if she could, that would be much nicer for all of us. We could have another quiet little celebration of Kit's engagement——"

" For God's sake! " Kit exclaimed.

" Yes, and all make friends again," Fanny went on even more warmly. " And Kit could move in here again until he goes to London. Yes, I think this is a wonderful idea! I'm sure Clare could work it. I couldn't, because if Laura said anything too damn stupid, I'd lose my temper and anyway she'd be so much on the defensive with me that she'd never

even let me get started. But she trusts Clare and she'd listen
to her."

"Oh dear," Clare said, "oh dear." She shrank back in
her chair, clutching the arms of it as if she were defying anyone to make her move from it. "I'm so tired, I'm so dreadfully tired."

"But, Clare, we'd all feel so much better if Laura came
to her senses," Fanny said. "You would too. There's nothing
like suspicion of other people for making one feel miserable,
and that's what wears one out."

"But I don't suspect anyone," Clare said, "of anything.
Of anything at all. My mind is an almost complete blank,
just faintly tinged with charity to all men. Please leave me
alone."

"No," Fanny said, her determination growing. "No,
this is a very good idea I've had. You go along now and
talk to her and do your best to bring her back with you.
I think if you're clever and give her a good way of backing
out of her own silly attitude without eating too much dirt,
she'll actually be glad to come."

"Send Basil," Clare suggested. "Men are so much better
at that sort of thing. Anyway, Basil is."

"No, you're the right person," Fanny said. "You
impressed her."

It took more argument, but Fanny, possessed with an idea,
developed an energy which it was difficult to oppose and
Clare's sheer tiredness seemed to make her particularly
defenceless against it. In the end it was obviously less of a
strain to yield and to go to see Laura than to go on arguing
any longer. Asking Kit to fetch her coat from her room, but
shaking her head absently when Basil suggested walking to
The Waggoners with her, she went out into the chilly dusk of
the evening.

As soon as she had gone, Fanny said to Kit, "There—
now we really can cheer up a bit. She'll probably work it,
you know. She's a clever creature."

Kit shook his head. "I don't think she'll work it."

"Why not?"

He shrugged his shoulders. "I just don't think so. Now

I'll go and pack a few of my things." He went to the door.
" By the way," he said, before going out, " have you any idea
where Jean Gregory got her money from? "

Fanny stared at him in amazement. " Good heavens,
why? "

" I don't know," he said in a troubled voice. " Laura saw
her from the window and wanted to know. I thought—
I thought from the way she asked that she'd met Jean before
somewhere, though I'm not sure about that."

" Well, so far as I know," Fanny said, " Jean got it in the
good old way, that's to say she inherited it from her parents."

" Are you sure about that? " Kit asked.

" Come to think of it, I don't think I ever asked her,"
Fanny said. " It isn't the sort of thing one does ask."

" No." Kit gave a curious sigh and went out.

Fanny turned quickly to Basil. " What in earth was that
about? " she asked.

" I haven't the faintest idea."

" I don't much like the sound of it."

" No," Basil said, " as a matter of fact, neither do I." He
came closer to the fire and stood looking down into it, his
bright eyes, that always looked so innocent and untroubled,
clouded for once with concern. " I rather wish you hadn't
made Clare go round to see Laura."

" But why? "

" She didn't want to go."

" Oh, Clare never wants to go anywhere. It's just her
neurosis! "

" It's necessary generally to be fairly tender with people's
neuroses, isn't it? If you aren't, they take it out on you or
on themselves afterwards. I thought she really did look as if
she were near a breaking-point. And there's something to
remember."

" What's that? "

" We've never found out why she wanted to meet Sir
Peter."

Fanny, lying back in her chair and looking up at Basil as
he stood there with the firelight flickering over his narrow,
dark face, raised her eyebrows in surprise. " No, nor we have.

But I haven't been thinking about it much. Have you? Have you really? "

" Off and on," he said.

" And you've thought of something? "

" No, nothing convincing."

" Well, I shouldn't think it's anything we need worry about," Fanny said, " not nearly as much, anyway, as this Kit and Laura business. What is that all about, Basil? What's going to happen to them? "

" They'll marry, I suppose."

" D'you know, I don't feel in the least convinced of that. I know you'll probably say I feel it simply because I don't want it to happen. All the same, something tells me that it won't happen. When two people are as little in love with each other as they are, how can it happen? "

" Then you think they aren't in love? "

" Of course not."

Basil turned his back on the fireplace, leant his shoulders against the crossbeam above it and looked contemplatively at Fanny.

" I shouldn't be surprised if you're right, after all," he said.

" I'm quite sure Kit isn't in love with Laura," she went on. " Now that I know what really happened between him and Susan that part of it is all quite easy to understand. He was absolutely confident of himself where Susan was concerned and then Susan turned him down, so he got engaged to Laura to prove to himself and to Susan that he could have someone much better than her if he wanted to. And I suppose it's a good deal my fault that he's the sort of person who'd do something as stupid and frightful as that—I got him so much into a habit of clinging to me that I got his self-confidence completely undermined, so that he had to do something really drastic when Susan hurt him. I expect you saw that all along, didn't you? "

" Well, in a way."

" Then why did you never say anything about it to me? "

" I very much doubt if you'd have paid any attention if I had," he said.

She thought that over for a moment, then nodded her head several times. "Yes—yes, I see what you mean. I'm an unreasonable type. I steam-roller people when they try to say things I don't want to listen to."

"Apart from that," he said, "I think it would have led to a quarrel between us and I—I couldn't have borne that."

She darted a questioning, disbelieving look at him. It almost seemed, from the way he had spoken, that there was no confidence in his heart that she loved him enough for a serious quarrel between them to be anything but totally destructive. It reminded her of something that she had sometimes suspected, that though he loved her with a quiet and intense concentration, he believed that the best of her love would never be his in return, but would always be reserved for her half-brother.

And heaven knows, Fanny thought, perhaps he had been right. Perhaps until recently, when she had felt Kit struggling against the protective entanglement of her love for him and had begun to ask herself scared and disturbing questions about what she had done to him.

Since that had started to happen, something unfamiliar had emerged in her feeling for Basil. She had become far more aware of him than before, and aware of her trust in him and her reliance on him.

"You shouldn't have worried," she said, "it wouldn't have done any damage."

"One can never be sure," he said.

"Yes, yes—though perhaps there wouldn't have been a quarrel at all. I'm not quarrelsome, am I? I don't quarrel much with people. I've managed never to quarrel with Tom Mordue, for instance."

"You're the sort of person who only quarrels with the people they care for," he answered.

"Then there's no need to worry about it, is there?"

"Except that that sort of quarrel sometimes goes deep— like this quarrel you're having with Kit. Where will that end?"

"It's over already, as far as I'm concerned," she said.

" Didn't I send Clare to fetch Laura, so that we could all make friends? I don't like Laura, and I can't understand why she should have made up her mind that she wants Kit, when, so far as I can see, she isn't in love with him, but if they're going to be married I'm not going to do anything to make difficulties for them. I'll see that Kit goes off to London with her and I'll go very, very carefully with him in future."

" I think it's easy enough to understand why Laura wants Kit," Basil said. " I think in her way she is in love with him. That's to say, I think she finds him attractive, and believes that she can make something of him. Apart from that, in spite of her good looks, she isn't really a particularly attractive young woman and she probably knows that by now. And she's thirtyish and she's got a child."

" Thirty is quite a normal marrying age for women nowadays," Fanny said, vaguely in defence of herself, since she had been a great deal older than that when she married Basil, " and I can think of lots of marriages where the woman already had one or more children."

" But I expect the women themselves were apprehensive beforehand, even if they had no reason to be."

" And inclined to clutch at straws? Well, if I were fairly successful in any career, like Laura, I'd certainly regard Kit as a straw, a very unsatisfactory straw."

" Because you simply can't remember that he's an attractive animal, although you've had plenty of chances to observe the results of that fact during the last two or three years."

" Susan evidently didn't think so——" She stopped as the telephone rang. " What's the betting that's Minnie," she said, " wanting to wail about something? You take it and say I'm out. I don't think I could take any of the Mordues at the moment."

Basil went to the telephone and picked it up.

As he did so, the door opened and Clare came into the room. She came in quietly and without looking at either Fanny or Basil, made straight for a chair by the fire. Jerking it a few inches nearer to the warmth, she sat down in it stiffly, holding her hands out to the blaze and staring intently into the heart of it with a wide, unblinking stare. Her face was extraordinarily pale.

Looking at her in surprise and with a sudden terrible sense of apprehension, Fanny asked sharply, " Whatever's happened? " She had been so startled by Clare's appearance that she forgot for the moment that Basil was at the telephone.

" I saw Laura," Clare said. Her voice dried up as she said it and she had to start again. " I saw Laura—and she won't come. I did my best, but nothing I could say would make her come."

CHAPTER SIXTEEN

WHEN KIT had left Laura in her room at The Waggoners, she had told him that she wanted to rest. She had shown him that she was tired. Dropping wearily on to the bed, kicking her shoes off, she had shut her eyes and yawned. Kit had added a piece of coal to the meagre fire that he had persuaded Mrs. Toles to light, then had gone out quietly.

Laura had lain quite still, her eyes still closed, until she heard his tread in the yard below, then she had sat up, reached hurriedly for the shoes that she had just discarded, and gone quickly downstairs.

She went to Mrs. Toles.

" Have you a telephone? " she asked.

" Yes, dear, through there," Mrs. Toles said, pointing at a door in a corner of the closed saloon bar.

Laura went to the door and found that it opened into a dark cupboard. The telephone was on a shelf with a local directory beside it. The cupboard was too dark for her to be able to look up the number she wanted, so she brought the directory out into the bar and standing under the light, started flicking over the pages. Mrs. Toles saw her there, then went back to the kitchen to finish her tea. She wondered if anything had happened between Kit Raven and his young lady. The girl, she thought, looked odd and excited.

In the Mordues' cottage the telephone rang. Minnie picked it up.

"Can I speak to Miss Mordue, please?" said a rather peremptory feminine voice.

Minnie did not recognise the voice, so she assumed that it belonged to someone connected with Susan's work.

"Hold on," she said. "I think she's home."

She went to the bottom of the staircase and called. There was no reply. After another call, she went back to the telephone.

"No, I'm sorry, she's not in," she said.

"Is that Mrs. Mordue speaking?" the voice asked.

"Yes," Minnie answered.

"Oh, Mrs. Mordue, this is Laura Greenslade speaking," the voice said. "I do so want to speak to your daughter. It's immensely important."

Minnie's hand, holding the telephone, trembled.

"Mrs. Greenslade?"

"Yes. Will she be home soon? I must speak to her."

"I'm expecting her any time," Minnie said. "She generally gets in about now. You're at the Lynams', I suppose. Couldn't she ring you when she gets in?"

"No, I'm not at the Lynams'," the voice said. "I'm at The Waggoners—and I want to catch the next train back to London, so I'll be leaving in a few minutes. But perhaps you could give your daughter a message from me. Would you do that, Mrs. Mordue?" There was an extraordinary urgency in the voice.

Minnie's heart began to beat faster. She had a premonition of what the message was to be.

"Of course, Mrs. Greenslade," she said. "Wait while I get a pencil and paper."

"No, that won't be necessary," the urgent, excited voice said. "Just say—just tell her that I know that Kit's really in love with her and not with me, and—and that I believe she's in love with Kit, and—and that I'd never want to stand between two people who love each other, and so I'm going back to London and I hope they'll both be very happy."

" But, Mrs. Greenslade—Laura—you can't just—I mean, I couldn't . . ."

While Minnie, in a voice now more excited than the other, fumbled for words, she heard a sound on the telephone that might have been a laugh, then the click as the connection was cut.

A laugh? No, it couldn't have been. It must have been a sob.

" Oh dear," Minnie said, standing there looking desperate and muddled. " Oh dear, the poor girl. She really shouldn't have . . . I mean, that isn't the way . . . Oh dear, how unhappy she must be. The poor girl. The poor girl."

" What the hell are you talking to yourself about now? " Tom asked, coming into the room.

Minnie stared at him unseeingly. His bald head bobbed across her vision without her being able to focus her thoughts upon him.

" And how can I say a thing like that to Susan? " she cried. " You know what Susan is."

" I do not," Tom said. " I do not know what anyone is, least of all Susan."

" She's proud and independent," Minnie said. " It's just the sort of thing to make her refuse ever to speak to him again. Oh, Tom, whatever shall I do? "

Tom Mordue sat down by the fire and picking up the morning's paper, rustled it ostentatiously.

" Leave me in peace, for one thing," he said.

" But, Tom, it's about Susan. It was that Greenslade girl. She says she's going back to London, and she's giving Kit up because she thinks he and Susan are in love with each other. And she wants me to tell Susan that."

Tom lowered his paper. He looked at Minnie hard and disbelievingly.

" You're making this up because it's what you want," he said.

Her wild, bewildered gaze met his. " It's what she said and then she gave a sob. It wrung my heart, Tom. Or— or was it a laugh? "

" Well, whatever it was, I'd say nothing about it to Susan,

if I were you," Tom said. " If Kit wants her, he can come
and ask for her—and I sincerely hope she'll say no to him
again, as she says now she did before. Young men who
don't know their minds for two days together aren't much
good to anyone, least of all when they're a present from
another woman, all done up in blue ribbon." He picked up
the paper again. " *I* always know my own mind."

" Yes, Tom," Minnie said abstractedly. " But she *is* in
love with him. I think—I think I'll at least tell her. . . .
I mean, I said I'd give the message. Or perhaps I should
ring up Fanny and ask her advice."

" For God's sake! " Tom shouted. " Can't anything be
done in this family without asking that woman's advice? "

" Tom! " Minnie said in a shocked voice.

He crumpled up the paper. " Oh, I'm sorry. I've nothing
against Fanny. But it's almost as bad as asking for charity,
this asking for advice, instead of using your own judgment.
I never ask for advice."

" No, Tom."

He turned his head, listening.

" There's Susan now," he said.

" I'll give her the message," Minnie said, " then *she* can
use her own judgment. That'll be best, won't it? "

She nodded her shaggy head, satisfied with her own
wisdom.

They heard Susan prop her bicycle against the wall below
the window and come in. While she was still in the little
hall, dragging off her gloves and blowing on her cold fingers,
Minnie called out to her. When Susan, listlessly inattentive,
made no answer, Minnie came hurrying out.

" There's just been a telephone message for you, dear,"
Minnie said, " from Laura Greenslade."

Susan frowned absently. Her small, square face looked
chilled by the cold wind and her eyes were preoccupied. She
was used to withdrawing herself from both her parents,
often only half-listening to what they were saying to one
another or to her, and now a moment passed before it
occurred to her that that what had been said was something
of interest. When it did, when the name of the person of

whom, as it happened, she was thinking, penetrated to her mind, she frowned harder than ever, so that her face for a moment bore a striking resemblance to her father's.

" What did you say? " she said sharply, almost as sharply as Tom might have said it.

Minnie gave a confused version of Laura's message.

A curiously anxious look came into Susan's eyes as she listened. She said nothing, but stood looking down at her hands, then in a quietly deliberate way she started pulling on her gloves again and in spite of the fact that they were old and shapeless, smoothed them very carefully over her fingers, staring at them hard as she did so. Then suddenly she put an arm round her mother's neck and kissed her, went quickly out of the house, took her bicycle, wheeled it along the garden path to the lane and set off towards the village.

At first she pedalled fast, feeling that it was of desperate importance that she should see Laura before she left to catch the train to London. She did not know what she wanted to say to her. In fact, it would be easiest, she thought, not to say anything at all but simply to slap Laura's face. Susan wished she had it in her to do that, instead of having to put her feelings into words. Words, in the experience of Tom Mordue's daughter, were treacherous things that generally created lasting havoc. From harmless little beginnings, they grew and grew in power and cruelty till everything within their range was destroyed. And she had no desire to destroy Laura. She did not even want to hurt her much. She only wanted . . .

What did she want? Did she or did she not want Kit?

Susan's pedalling grew slower. She found herself thinking less of Laura and more of Kit. She was, of course, in love with him. In spite of the extraordinary emotional crudity and stupidity of his treatment of both herself and Laura, she was deeply in love with him. And knowing at last for sure that she was in love with him, and thinking of herself as something worse than emotionally crude and stupid, she had been bitterly miserable during the last two weeks. She had not believed for a moment that she could get him back. Even after they had met at Fanny's party, and she had seen quite clearly that his engagement to Laura had given him little happiness, Susan had not believed that there was any way of stopping him proceeding with it. Having lived all her life close to Tom Mordue, it was perhaps natural for her to take for granted that when a man had made up his mind to do something truly preposterous, there was no way of saving him from himself.

But now Laura was tossing him back at her.

Susan had not yet met Laura. She had only seen her photograph and heard Fanny talk about her, and now the remarkable message that had come by telephone had reached Susan only through her mother, so that she had not even heard Laura's voice. She did not know precisely what had been said, or in what tone the message had been given. Her mother had told her that Laura had sounded very excited, but Susan did not think of Minnie as a reliable reporter, and one doubt haunted Susan now, that in fact some sort of vicious joke was being played upon her. Pedalling her bicycle more and more slowly, she found herself thinking of that job that Colin Gregory had tried to make her take, found herself wondering if perhaps it was still open.

In the village street she saw Jean Gregory.

Jean was standing in front of The Waggoners, looking up and down the street, and for a moment Susan had a distinct impression that she was looking up and down to see whether anyone was watching her.

It was a curious impression to have. There could be few people so unlikely to be acting in such a fashion as Jean Gregory. There could be few people with so little reason in their lives ever to need to act furtively. Yet as Susan applied her brakes, jumped off her bicycle and wheeled it towards Jean, she felt that Jean had been startled by her appearance, was put out by it and quite at a loss.

Susan told her at once, " I've come to see Laura Green-slade."

" *You* have? " Jean said, emphasising the word so oddly that it sounded as if what she was really saying was, " You have *too?* "

It made Susan ask, " Then are you going to see her? "

"Oh no—no," Jean said. "As a matter of fact, I—I was just going into The Waggoners to see if Colin's there."

Susan's mind was filled with her own concerns and she did not trouble to ask herself why Jean should lie to her, as lying she certainly was, for even Jean, quietly puritan though she might be, would scarcely have been looking up and down the street in that furtive way merely to make sure that no one should see her going into The Waggoners. Leaning her bicycle against the wall, Susan pushed at the door of the saloon bar, leaving it to Jean whether to follow her in or not.

For a moment Jean did not move, then with a shrug of the shoulders and a hesitant, undecided air, she followed Susan through the door.

Susan was asking Mrs. Toles where she could find Mrs. Greenslade. The only other person in the room was Fred Davin, the ironmonger. He was in his usual place at the bar, with a pint mug in front of him. He said good evening to Jean, which made Susan, who had not heard her come in, aware that she was there. Turning to glance at her, Susan was surprised to see Jean's extreme pallor. In the darkness outside it had not been noticeable, but now, in the lighted room, Jean's face looked so drawn and grey that Susan thought she must be feeling ill. If that were so, it explained Jean's unusual behaviour in the street. If she had suddenly felt faint, she might have been looking up and down for someone who could help her.

"Are you all right, Jean?" Susan asked anxiously.

Jean's eyes were feverishly bright and at the same time vacant.

"Yes, I'm quite all right," she said, as if the question surprised her. "Mrs. Toles, have you seen my husband?"

"No, dear, not since morning," Mrs. Toles answered.

"I think—I think I'll sit down and wait for him, if you don't mind," Jean said. "I said I'd join him here."

"That's right, dear, sit down and make yourself comfortable." Mrs. Toles then turned her attention back to Susan. "I think you'll find her there, Miss Mordue. She hasn't said anything to me about leaving, but it's true her room isn't very grand, as I said to Mr. Raven, and maybe she isn't satisfied. I said to Mr. Raven, 'The room isn't very grand, Mr. Raven,' I said, ' but she's welcome to it, only don't blame me if she isn't satisfied,' I said——"

" Thanks," Susan said and went through the door and started up the stairs.

On the chair on to which Jean had sunk, rather as if her feet would no longer carry her, she sat looking isolated, lost in herself and utterly out of place. She must have been very cold, for she was trembling slightly.

Seeing this, Fred Davin said, " Why not come nearer the fire, Mrs. Gregory ? "

She started to turn her head to look at him.

At that moment, from upstairs, there came a scream.

Of the three people in the saloon bar, Jean moved the fastest. It was almost as if she had been waiting for the sound. While Mrs. Toles was still pressing a hand to her heart and Fred Davin was looking round in an incredulous way, as if a scream in The Waggoners were so far from the course of nature that probably it had not really happened at all, Jean crossed to the door through which Susan had gone, tore it open and started to run up the stairs.

But she was only on the third stair when Susan, looking ill with fright and horror, came racing down. Stumbling against Jean and catching hold of her shoulder to save herself, she almost made Jean fall.

" Don't go up there—don't! " Susan cried. " It's horrible ! "

Jean drew away from her. Her muddled and undecided air had vanished, her trembling had stopped. She gave a searching look into Susan's terrified eyes, then started again up the stairs.

Susan clutched her arm.

" Don't—you can't go in there, Jean! " she sobbed. " She's—she's dead! "

" Laura Greenslade ? " Jean said.

Mrs. Toles and Fred Davin by now were also in the narrow passage at the foot of the stairs.

They heard Susan say, " Yes, and there's the handle of the

knife sticking out of her back and there's blood all over her
—she's been *murdered*, Jean!"

Jean shook herself free of Susan's hand and went on up
the stairs.

Fred Davin called to her to come back, saying that he
would go up.

"I'm a nurse," Jean answered austerely, "I've seen such
things before."

Following her, Fred Davin entered Laura's bedroom only
a moment after her.

He found Jean standing quite still, looking down at the
body of Laura Greenslade, which was sprawled face down-
wards on the highly polished linoleum. Laura's dark hair
had come loose and was tumbled about her head. Her hands
looked as if they were reaching out to grasp something. The
horn handle of a knife stood out between her shoulder blades.
A great patch of her tweed jacket was soaked in blood. In
the fireplace the fire that she had ordered was burning
cheerfully.

As Fred Davin stood there, he saw Jean stoop as if she
were about to touch the handle of the knife.

"We didn't ought to touch anything, Mrs. Gregory," he
said.

"No," Jean said, "of course not." But she remained
stooping, peering down at the little that she could see of
Laura's face, under the tumbled hair. Then she slowly
straightened up and turned to the door.

"We'll have to call the police," she said.

"But who done it?" Fred Davin said, as if she could
tell him. "Not Mr. Raven. He never done a thing like
that."

"No," Jean said.

She went out of the room and down the stairs.

In the bar Mrs. Toles was treating Susan and herself to
brandy. Without asking Jean and Fred Davin if they wanted
it, she filled glasses for them too. Jean gave a slight shake of
her head as Mrs. Toles pushed one of them towards her.

"There, dear, you drink it up," Mrs. Toles insisted. "I
wouldn't have gone up there like you did, not if you was to

pay me to do it, not after what Miss Mordue's been telling me. You drink it up."

Again Jean shook her head. She looked at Susan.

"She's dead," Jean said. "There isn't any doubt of it."

"I know there isn't. I—I looked," Susan said.

"You mean you touched her?"

"No, I—I don't think I did." Susan sounded dazed. "But with all that blood . . . I'm going to ring Mummy up." She looked round. "Where's the telephone, Mrs. Toles?"

She sounded like a child who in time of trouble thinks first of telling her mother.

"In that cupboard over there, dear," Mrs. Toles said, as she had said earlier to Laura.

Fred Davin had swallowed his brandy.

"I'll be going for the police now, Mrs. Toles," he said, "if you ladies aren't nervous being left on your own. If you are, I'll call in Mr. Crowfoot from next door."

"No, Mr. Davin, we'll be all right, thank you—but don't be long," Mrs. Toles said bravely, reaching again for the brandy bottle. "The poor young lady—of all terrible things! And who's going to tell poor Mr. Raven?"

"I will," Susan muttered, going towards the telephone. "I'll ring up the Lynams. They'll tell him. And I'll ring up my mother. . . ."

She went into the cupboard, found a switch that worked a dim light inside it, closed the door on herself, and picked up the telephone.

She rang up first her home and then the Lynams. She spoke briefly and fairly collectedly to her mother and afterwards to Basil. As she put the telephone down, her glance was held by a white shape on the floor. Without thinking much of what she was doing, she bent to pick it up.

It was an envelope, addressed to Mrs. Charles Greenslade. It was an old envelope, fairly crumpled, as if it had been in a handbag or a pocket for some time. There was nothing inside it, but on one corner of it, in pencil, were two numbers. Each number had some meaning for Susan, for the first was the Mordues' telephone number and the second was that of the Gregorys'.

Susan hesitated there inside the cupboard. It seemed certain to her, looking at those numbers, that Laura had telephoned Jean as well as herself. That probably meant that Laura had asked Jean to come to see her, or else that because of something that Laura had said, Jean had decided on her own to come. It had been with the intention of seeing Laura that Jean had waited outside The Waggoners, waiting furtively, looking up and down the street, hoping not to be seen.

Or, Susan thought, her heart suddenly thumping, had Jean already seen Laura when she arrived on her bicycle? *Had Jean been leaving The Waggoners?*

Thrusting the envelope into her pocket, she decided that she would not let anyone see it until she had shown it to Jean herself and given her a chance to explain. Switching off the light in the cupboard, she emerged into the bar and looked round for Jean.

But Jean had gone.

CHAPTER SEVENTEEN

As Basil put the telephone down, after speaking to Susan, he turned and looked thoughtfully at Clare. She had sat down stiffly on the edge of a chair and was holding her hands out to the fire.

" Clare," he said gently, " what's the truth about this? "

She lowered her head a little, so that less could be seen of her face, and said, " The truth about what? "

" About what happened when you went to see Laura."

" I saw her——"

" Alive or dead? "

Fanny gave a cry. Her face became almost as pale, as distorted as in the reflection in the old gilt-framed mirror. " *Dead*, Basil? "

" That's what Susan says. Stabbed in the back, in her own room at The Waggoners. Susan found her."

" She was alive when I saw her," Clare said woodenly.

" And I told her you wanted to make friends with her and I asked her to come back with me, but she refused. That's all."

Basil went to the door.

Fanny asked quickly, " Where are you going? "

" To find Kit," he said and went out.

Fanny stared after him blankly, not yet able to take in what had happened. Then she turned on Clare. For once Fanny looked angry.

" You aren't telling the truth, Clare. From the first you haven't told the truth and one's only got to look at you now to know that you're lying. What happened? What happened really? "

Clare did not reply. Sitting there rigidly, she had taken on an air of intense thought.

" Clare! " Fanny said loudly.

Clare's quick frown made her look as she did when she was interrupted in her work. She seemed to be trying to blot out her own knowledge that there was anyone else in the room.

Fanny strode heavily across the room and stood over her.

" Clare, will you tell the truth about what you found there? "

Absently, Clare answered, " She was dead, of course."

" *Of course?* Then why did you try to pretend she was alive when you saw her? What's happening to you? "

" Yes, she was dead," Clare said thoughtfully, as if she were working it out as she went along. " She was dead. And discovering her was a profoundly upsetting experience. I doubt if I have ever had such a shock in my life. I left quietly, hoping that I could avoid becoming involved in the affair. However, since you say it was obvious to you at once that I was lying when I said that I found her alive, I see that it will probably be best if I admit that I found her dead. Yes—dead." Her repetition of the word had the sound of an experiment, as if she were listening to see how she liked it.

Cold had invaded Fanny's body. She was aware of it in her hands and her feet and along her spine. She felt it strangely at the top of her head, from where the chill seemed to be spreading into her brain.

" You're still lying," she said.

" No, I'm speaking the truth."

" Then—something's happened to you."

" Yes, indeed. I've had a very great shock."

Footsteps on the stairs made Fanny aware that Kit and Basil were coming down together. She went to the door and saw Kit go by. He gave her a look, but he did not pause. Basil, putting a hand on Fanny's shoulder, guided her back into the sitting-room.

" Shouldn't you have gone with him? " she asked.

" He wanted to go alone," Basil said.

Clare was still sitting in the same position by the fire. Basil looked at her, then questioningly at Fanny.

" She says now that she found Laura dead," Fanny said.

" Yes, of course," Basil said.

" Of course," Clare echoed.

" But then——" Fanny began, but broke off as Basil very slightly shook his head.

He stood still in the middle of the room, frowning at the floor, as if he were considering a plan of action. When Fanny started to speak again, he again shook his head. Clare also remained still. It almost seemed, Fanny thought, that to the three people in the room Laura's death required no comment. At last she could not endure the silence a moment longer.

" Whatever's happened to you both? " she cried. " What are you doing? "

" In our different ways," Basil answered, " we are both trying to think. Quickly, if possible."

" You mean before the police get here? "

" That, I imagine, is Clare's problem," he said. " Mine—mine is more difficult."

" I don't understand you," Fanny said.

" Well, now that it's apparent that Laura was the intended victim of our poisoning, the question is . . ."

He stopped, as a knock sounded on the front door.

" Is that the police now? " Fanny asked, looking appre-
hensively at Clare.

" I'll see," Basil said, but Clare did not stir or give any
sign of even having heard the knocking.

In a moment Basil returned, not with the police, but with
Colin Gregory. As they came into the room, Basil was
telling Colin what had happened. Fanny felt quite unable to
let Basil tell the story by himself, and broke in, telling it in
almost the same words, but a moment after him. Clare did
not even glance in Colin's direction, but still sat stiffly,
communing with the fire.

Whether it was because this behaviour of hers struck Colin
as excessively strange, or because of something else in his
mind, he seemed unable, while Basil and Fanny were
speaking, to take his eyes from Clare. When the story was
told, he said nothing for a moment, then made a little gesture
of helplessness, as if he could really find nothing to say.

Then he said, " By the way, I suppose Jean hasn't been
here since I left? "

" No," Fanny said.

He muttered something and turned to the door.

" Why? " Fanny asked quickly. " What's the matter,
Colin? "

" Nothing," he said. " Nothing, I'm sure. I just thought
she might be here. But since she isn't——"

Another knock on the door interrupted him.

Again Fanny exclaimed, " That's the police now! "

But this time it was the Mordues.

They came in with Minnie for once in advance of Tom.
She was filled with passion of some sort. Her bony, slack
body was taut with it, so that she looked some inches taller
than usual. Her eyes were ablaze.

" Ah," she said, seeing Colin, " the man I want! "

Tom, staying in her wake, as if he half hoped to be able
to remain hidden behind her, looked shrunken and scared.

" It's her idea, Fanny," he said. " I don't want to make
trouble of any kind."

Minnie looked wildly round. " That man Colin," she said,
" I went to his house and they told me he'd just come here.

And it's better like this, because I can say what I want in front of impartial witnesses."

" Yes, Minnie dear," Colin said quietly. But he edged towards the door, still in a hurry to go in search of Jean.

Minnie took a deep breath, as if she were about to plunge into a stormy sea and swim for her life. Then dropping at once into her usual mild and flustered manner of speaking, she said, " Well, Colin, as soon as I heard from Susan what had happened, I thought there's something I've got to do at once and that's see you. Because I knew that as soon as you heard too, you'd be sticking your nose in and interfering. For some reason, for the last week or two, you've done nothing but interfere in the affairs of my family." Her voice was rising slightly. Some of her rage was returning, though it was plain that face to face with Colin she found it difficult to go on being as angry with him as she had thought she was. " What I want you to understand," she went on, " is that I will not have you going to the police and remarking, in that insinuating way of yours, how strange it was that Susan should have gone to see Laura. I want to make sure that Fanny and Basil keep you here until I've talked to the police and told them myself why Susan went to see Laura."

" Don't you think she's capable of telling them that herself? " Colin asked.

His voice was as quiet as before, but he looked more disturbed. He was not looking at Minnie as he spoke, however, but again at Clare, sitting stiff and still by the fire, taking no notice of the fact that several people had come into the room. But whether the concern in Colin's eyes was because of Minnie's words or Clare's silence, it was impossible to tell.

Minnie went on: " If Susan's left alone, without interference from you, she'll be all right. But after the way you came out to see us, threatening Tom with all sorts of things, I don't know what you may be capable of next."

" I wasn't threatening any of you, Minnie," Colin said. " I came to find something out, that's all."

" You threatened us," Minnie repeated stubbornly. " You threatened Tom and me. You made up a wonderful story about how Tom and I between us killed Sir Peter Poulter.

And then you said that if anything more happened that could hurt the Lynams, you'd take this story to the police."

" And is that why you're here now, Minnie? " Colin asked. " Something more has happened and you think this is the time I'll go to the police with that story? "

Tom had just gulped a drink that Basil had given him.

" I'm not afraid," he said. " I'm not in the least afraid. It was Minnie's idea, having things out like this. I'm all for speaking one's mind when it's necessary, but still I always like to avoid trouble when I can. You all know I do."

" Of course you do, Tom," Colin said. " You're the most peace-loving man in the village. And I'm sorry if you think I'm threatening you. All I really wanted, as I said just now, was a small piece of information. And in a perhaps unscrupulous way, I got it."

" I accept the word unscrupulous," Tom said.

" I got the information," Colin said, " that it was Susan who had turned Kit down and not the other way round, as most of us thought. And that meant that even you, Tom, hadn't the shadow of a reason for a grudge against the Lynams. So one of my theories about the way that Sir Peter might have died collapsed. But I had to test it before—before I began to think too much about my other theory."

" Had to? " Tom said. " You had to, indeed? " The old excitable shrillness was back in his voice. It was as if Colin's admission that his theory had collapsed had relieved Tom of the fears that had been keeping a brake on his temper. " You aren't a person who recognises many duties. The truth is—and there's nothing I'll say about a man behind his back that I won't say to his face—the truth is that you hadn't got to do anything at all. The police are capable and intelligent men, which means that there was never any sort of compulsion on you to go sticking your nose into the affairs of my family."

" Yes, capable and intelligent men," Minnie said, sounding proud of Tom for having produced the phrase. " And let me tell you, too, that Tom and I have been at home together all day—until that telephone call came from Susan. So you can't even begin to make out a case that either of us had anything to do with that poor woman's death. And as for Susan herself . . ."

"Yes," Colin said, "while we're at it, what about Susan?"

"She went to see Mrs. Greenslade," Minnie said, "because Mrs. Greenslade rang up and said she had come to the conclusion that Kit was really in love with Susan and she thought Susan was in love with Kit, and she herself would never want to stand between two people who were in love with each other, so she was going to give him up and go back to London."

"*Laura* said that?" Fanny exclaimed incredulously. "*Laura* did?"

Minnie gave a solemn nod. "She said it to me myself. Susan wasn't home yet, so she said it to me and asked me to tell Susan. I think she must have been a very fine young woman. I wish we'd had the chance to become friends with her. Still, Susan felt, of course, that that wasn't the kind of thing one could settle just like that on the telephone, so she jumped on her bicycle and went to see her. And she found her dead—murdered!"

"She spoke to you, Minnie?" Fanny said thoughtfully.

"She did," Minnie said, "and I can remember every word she said."

"And that's the only time you've heard her speak, isn't it?" Fanny asked.

"Yes, I'm sorry to say it is."

"Then," Fanny said excitedly, "at least we know one thing. One thing only. Laura's murderer was a woman."

Tom and Minnie exchanged glances, then Tom said, "How d'you make that out, Fanny?"

"Because of the voice, the woman's voice on the telephone," Fanny said. "Because it's obvious it wasn't Laura who spoke to Minnie. Laura would never have said a thing like that. Never in this world. She wasn't the person to give up anyone or anything. The whole idea's preposterous. No, it's perfectly clear that the person who rang Minnie up, saying she was Laura, wasn't Laura at all, but the person who'd just murdered Laura, and knowing that Susan would be an easy person to shift suspicion on to, made sure that she

should arrive on the spot. Of course that's what happened.
. . ." The hurried, confident sentences stopped. Fanny took
one swift, horrified glance round the room, careful not to
let her eyes rest on anyone, least of all that stiff and silent
figure by the fire. Then she turned to Basil and clutched at
his arm. Under her breath, she said, " But why? . . . No,
it can't be. There isn't any reason."

Colin said, " There's a very good reason, Fanny."

She started and gazed at him disbelievingly.

He gave a sigh that sounded terribly tired and discouraged.
Then he walked to the window, where Laura's photograph
still stood, and for a moment looked down in silence into the
beautiful, empty face.

" There's a very good reason," he said in a low voice,
" but we'll come to that in a minute. First let's talk about
phenylthiourea."

There was a stir of surprise in the room, as if the complete
change in Colin's tone had affected everyone unexpectedly.
Basil particularly looked startled, and an expression of intense
curiosity, as if he could not quite believe in what was happening, appeared on his thin, dark face.

Colin went on without any sound of enthusiasm for what he
had to say, while he slid one finger-nail along the frame that
contained the photograph.

" The strange bitter taste of the lobster and the extraordinary fact that there were two people here who couldn't
taste certain bitter things have been the real red herrings in
the case," he said   " The word phenylthiourea has been
dragged across the trail again and again. The suggestion is
that somebody knew that either Mrs. Greenslade or Sir
Peter couldn't taste phenylthiourea, and therefore, when
presented with lobster that was heavily flavoured with it,
and spiced with enough arsenic to kill a horse, would eat it
without any misgivings, though no one else would touch the
terrible stuff. Well . . ." He drawled the word a little. " I
suppose it *could* happen like that. Someone could think of
doing a murder in that way. But I should have said there'd
have been just about ninety-nine chances in a hundred against
its success. Think of all the things that could have gone

wrong with the scheme. First, as appears to have been the case here, there might have been more than one person who couldn't taste phenylthiourea, so that more than one person might have died. I don't say that that would necessarily have distressed our murderer. . . ."

"May I say," Basil interrupted, "that that was a highly unlikely thing to happen. It did happen, as unlikely things sometimes do. But the murderer might almost have been justified, I think, in calculating that it would not happen."

Colin's voice was sardonic. "That's from the man who's used to handling statistics in a scientific fashion. In my own earthier way, I think the murderer was taking a hell of a risk of committing wholesale slaughter. However, he was taking one even greater risk, from his point of view, which was that the poisoned lobster wouldn't be eaten at all. If a lot of people around one start saying that something tastes bad, it's a quite natural thing to get apprehensive, even if one can't taste anything bad oneself. So, as you probably realise by now, I'm perfectly convinced that that was not the method used by our murderer. In fact, I don't believe that there was any phenylthiourea or any arsenic in the lobster."

There was a murmur in the room. It had a sound of doubt, almost of consternation in it. At the same time, it had an undertone of assent.

Minnie said, "But why do you keep on talking as if we weren't sure still which of those two was meant to be murdered?"

"But are we sure?" Colin asked.

"Of course we are," she said. "It was poor Mrs. Grenslade. He—or is it really she, like Fanny said?—missed the first time, so made sure of it, the monster, this afternoon."

"I don't think so," Colin said. "I really don't think so. But I think that's just what we were meant to think."

He paused, turning his back on the photograph, looking round at them all.

No one spoke, so he went on, picking his words carefully: "I mean that Laura's murder, like Laura's queer inability to taste phenylthiourea, was an enormous red herring. She died because she insisted on thrusting herself forward as a

victim. All the murderer had to do, when Laura herself had
prepared the scene for him so well, was to go ahead and
kill her. Then he could be almost certain that the highly
successful murder of Sir Peter Poulter would always be looked
on as a mistake and the real method and the real murder
never discovered."

For the first time for many minutes Clare Forwood stirred.
Lifting her head, she looked directly, but with a stunned,
blank gaze, at Colin.

His next words were addressed to her. He spoke quietly
and gently.

"That's true, isn't it, Miss Forwood? There wasn't any
arsenic in the lobster. You wouldn't have risked harming
your old friends. You went into the kitchen, and added
something bitter to the lobster, because you knew of Sir
Peter's inability to taste certain things and you thought
that if he ate a few of the patties which were refused by
other people, no one would even think about the cocktail
which really contained the poison. I wasn't here myself, but
I've been told by two or three people that you spent a good
deal of the evening talking to Sir Peter. So it was easy for
you, wasn't it? Quite easy and simple and practical, not
like all this fantastic messing about with phenylthiourea."

Stiffly Clare started to stand up. From the way she stared
at Colin, it might have been thought that she was seeing not
merely one man, but a whole army of the law closing in
upon her. Her face was grey and the skin of it seemed to
have shrunk close to the skull, so that it looked all jutting,
heavy forehead and small, fierce jawbone.

In a low, precise voice, as penetrating as that of an ex-
perienced governess quelling a troublesome class, she said,
"*I hate people!*"

Then she collapsed in a dead faint.

CHAPTER EIGHTEEN

FANNY RAN TO Clare, but as she knelt beside her, became suddenly uncertain what to do. She did not feel sure that it would be either wise or kind to bring Clare back to consciousness at that moment.

Colin's face was drawn. He seemed to be finding it harder to bear the results of what he had done than he expected.

"The resemblance," he muttered. "Don't you all see the resemblance?"

Basil said, "Yes, it shows now, doesn't it? The forehead, the eyebrows . . . She's very like him. It was clever of you to notice that, Colin. Or had you anything else to go on?"

"No," Colin said. "But I noticed the resemblance at once when I saw a photograph of Sir Peter in a newspaper after his death. It could easily have been a photograph of Miss Forwood."

"I never noticed it," Fanny said. "I never noticed any resemblance."

"You know her too well," Colin said.

"And you mean," she said shakily, "that Clare was related to him?"

"I think he was her father," Colin said. "Remember, Fanny, it was you who always said that Clare wasn't really interested in anyone but the members of her own family, and that she never wrote about anyone but the members of her own family. So it was easy to argue from that that if she took a strong and surprising interest in someone, that person was in some way connected with her family. And then there was the resemblance."

"But why should that make her want to murder him?" Minnie demanded.

"You'll find that out later," Colin replied. "It may have been revenge for the dishonour done to the man she had believed was her father and whom no doubt she had loved.

Or it may have been hatred because of Sir Peter's neglect of her. There's no need to look for an altogether sane motive."

"D'you think he knew that he was her father?" Fanny asked.

"I don't know," Colin said.

"If he did, then he did neglect her."

"Wouldn't that have been the best thing to do, in the circumstances? He had a family of his own and so had Alice Forwood."

Clare's head stirred a little and her lips seemed to be forming one or two inaudible words, but her eyes did not open.

"Let's get her up to her room and put her to bed," Fanny said. "And Basil can telephone for Dr. McLean. Or—or perhaps Colin would—would go and fetch him."

He gave her a grave, unhappy look, as if he realised quite clearly that at that moment Fanny could scarcely bear to have him in the house.

"Yes, Fanny, of course I'll go," he said.

"But what about Sir Peter's servants," Minnie exclaimed. "We heard this afternoon that they'd been arrested."

"If they were," Colin said, as he went to the door, "they'll have perfect alibis for Laura's murder."

He went out into the passage and out into the small garden. The dimly lit village street had a dreadful busyness, with several cars drawn up in front of The Waggoners and far too many people for that time of the evening standing about in groups. Colin was at the gate when the door behind him opened once more and Fanny came out.

"Colin, I—I didn't mean . . ." she began.

"It's all right," he said. "I know how you're feeling about me at the moment."

"No," she said, "no, I'm not. It's only that this—it's a terrible shock. Clare's my very oldest friend. And though she's so queer and difficult to get on with, I admire her more than anyone I know."

"Of course, Fanny," Colin said.

"And I still only half-believe what you said is true."

"Then perhaps it'll turn out I'm wrong after all."

" Perhaps." There was not much conviction in her tone.
" But nothing will ever be the same again."

He laid a hand on her shoulder.

" Just wait," he said.

" It won't do any good," she answered miserably.

" Everything gets forgotten, Fanny."

" No, nothing will ever be the same again," she said.

" It's got to be! " He spoke with a note of passion in his
voice that startled Fanny. " Things were too good to let
them get spoilt. We've got to forget it all." As he said it, he
glanced up at the lights of his home.

There was a light in the window of Jean's little office.

" Jean's home," he said. He went through the gate and
started walking towards the house.

" Colin—aren't you going for Dr. McLean? " Fanny called
after him.

He wheeled round and started walking in the opposite
direction.

" Sorry," he said, " I was just thinking of something else."

Fanny stood watching him for a moment, then went
indoors.

She found that Basil and Tom between them had carried
Clare up to her bedroom. She was lying on the bed while
Minnie bustled about the room, loosening Clare's clothing,
switching on the heater, drawing curtains.

Fanny went to the foot of the bed and stood looking down
at the small blanched face on the pillow, seeing the resemblance to Sir Peter so clearly now that she wondered how she
could possibly have missed it earlier. Particularly the remarkable foreheads were alike She remembered the two of them
sitting side by side in the corner of the room, the old man,
ill and exhausted by life, scarcely troubling any more to
keep any hold upon it, yet still able to simulate a vivid interest
in it, and the small, middle-aged woman who had withdrawn
from life as fully as she was able years ago, except that her
curious, brilliant mind still struggled to penetrate certain of
its smaller mysteries. The old man had lost his wife and his
sons. The woman had never had husband or children, and
had lost parents and brothers. What might the two of them,

intimately related to one another as they were, have meant
to one another if death had not struck?

Fanny shivered.   She wondered for how long Clare had
known of her relationship to Sir Peter Poulter?   She had
spoken to Fanny many times of her mother's lovers, usually
in a tone more admiring than bitter, but never as if she had
any doubts that Arthur Forwood was the father of her mother's
children.   Clare had been deeply attached to this supposed
father of hers, though she had always felt that she was of no
great importance to him and that her brothers, both younger
than herself, had the whole of his affection.   She had had a
great love for one of her brothers and an almost equal detesta-
tion for the other, but apart from these emotions, called forth
at least to some extent by their qualities, had always been
oppressed by a helpless jealousy of them both.   They had
been equally jealous of her, because of their brilliant mother's
obvious preference for her.   These relationships, these jealousies
and grudges and smothered miseries, had been the material
of all Clare's writing.

And then she had discovered that she had another father
who had withheld his affection from her even more completely than the one she had known.

Fanny leant forward suddenly, peering at the shrunken
face.   It had just occurred to her that Clare was no longer
unconscious.   If Minnie would leave the room, she thought,
Clare would probably show signs of recovery.

" Minnie," Fanny said, " there's some brandy downstairs.
Basil said he was going to bring it, but something must have
stopped him.   Could you go and find him?   I think I ought
to stay with Clare."

Minnie nodded and went tiptoeing out of the room.

As soon as the door had closed Clare opened her eyes,
glanced round, made sure that she and Fanny were alone,
then beckoned Fanny towards her.

In a fierce whisper Clare said, " Listen, Fanny, you've got
to help me.   You've got to do something for me.   Will you
do it?   Will you promise? "

Her eyes looked dreadfully brilliant.   Though she was
conscious, she was not normal.

"Promise!" she repeated frantically.

"All right, Clare," Fanny said softly. "What do you want me to do?"

"Keep people away from me for a little while. Give me a little time, just a little. Don't let anyone come in."

"All right," Fanny said. "I'll do my best."

"You too," Clare said, "I mean you too. Go away and leave me quite to myself for a little while."

"But, Clare——"

"Please!"

On the staircase there was a sound of footsteps. Fanny knew that they were Basil's and more than anything else just then she wanted him to come in.

But Clare, hearing the footsteps, exclaimed in agony, "Please, Fanny, please—keep them away from me! For just a little!"

Fanny drew away from her. Softly she went to the door, opened it only just far enough to let herself out, closed it behind her and went along the passage. As she did so, she heard a thump as Clare leapt out of bed, rushed to the door and locked herself in.

When Basil reached the top of the stairs, he found Fanny standing there, leaning against the wall. She was trembling violently.

He put down the tray that he had been carrying and put his arms round her. Her trembling went on and she clung to him tensely. For a moment she could not speak at all, then, as he glanced past her to the closed door of Clare's room, she managed to say in his ear, "I left her alone. She begged me to, Basil. She begged it. We're old friends, Basil. Could I have done anything else?"

"No," he said, "I don't think so."

His voice was curiously unperturbed. For once his calm seemed to Fanny a shocking thing. She wondered if it was possible that he had not understood what she meant.

"Basil, I left her *alone*—don't you understand?"

"Yes," he said, "poor woman, I can quite understand her feelings. She really does hate people and after what she's

been through to-day I should think she'd find it utterly
necessary to be quite alone."

" Basil——"

" My dear, if you're thinking that she's taking her own
life at the moment," he said, " you've no need whatever
to worry. Clare wants to go on living to write a lot more
books."

" But when the police come——"

" But, darling Fanny, you don't believe she did it, do
you? "

She drew away from him. She looked searchingly into his
face, a look which he returned with one of mild, innocent
surprise. Then he gave her a little shake.

" Clare would never murder anyone," he said. " You
ought to know that. She's collapsed because life has been
altogether too much for her just lately. You have to remember
that she really does hate people—even you, when she's seen
too much of you, though the rest of the time she loves you
dearly. And she's had to be among people for days on end.
Not to mention finding a body and being accused of murder.
I expect she'll now have a mild nervous breakdown, then
become her own normal peculiar self."

" But then," Fanny cried, feeling that she would have to
start laughing or crying, but that it would be wrong to do
either, " who did kill the Poulter man and Laura? "

" Someone who didn't come to the party," Basil answered.

" I don't understand," she said.

" Think," he said. " about the phenylthiourea."

" No," she cried, as if the thought of doing such a thing
maddened her. " No—I tell you, I don't understand."

" Well, let's go downstairs," he said, " and leave Clare
in peace for a little, as she wanted, and I'll tell you how
things strike me. Not that I understand the whole situation
by any means. But I think I do understand about the
phenylthiourea."

Picking up the tray with the bottle of brandy on it, he
started down the stairs.

Tom and Minnie were still in the sitting-room and had
been joined by Susan. Tom's arm was round her, looking a

little inexperienced and uncomfortable in that position, and he was patting her gently and saying, "Never mind, dear, never mind—we'll go home now and Mummy will put you to bed. You'll soon get over it."

Susan did not look in the least as if she wanted to be put to bed. She had got over the worst of the shock of discovering Laura, and though her small, square face was sombre, it was no longer abnormally pale. Her eyes were alert.

"Fanny, please, there's something I want to know," she said, as soon as Fanny and Basil came into the room. "Can you tell me . . . ?"

But Fanny, glancing round the room, interrupted her. "Where's Kit? Didn't you see him, Susan?"

"He's with the police," Susan said. "They're asking him an awful lot of questions. But listen, can you tell me——?"

"Will he be back soon?" Fanny asked.

"I don't know. Please, Fanny, do tell me, do you know anything about where Jean's money came from?"

Fanny frowned at the question, while Tom said, "Well, I'm damned!" and Minnie said, "Good gracious me!" No one made any attempt to answer the question.

Susan clenched her hands in a gesture of extreme impatience.

"Please!" she exclaimed. "Doesn't anybody know?"

"You know, Kit asked me that this afternoon," Fanny said, "but he didn't tell me why he wanted to know. Has he told you, Susan?"

"Yes," Susan said, "and put together with what I know it sounds completely crazy. You see, when he took Laura to The Waggoners this morning, she happened to look out of the window and she saw Jean. And she got awfully excited at seeing her and wanted to know who she was. And when Kit said that she was Jean Gregory, who lived next door to you, Laura got more excited still, and said, 'She's rich, isn't she? She's rich!' And Kit says that all through the afternoon Laura kept asking him questions about Jean, about how rich she was and how the Gregorys lived—that's to say, was she really *rich*, or just a little better off than most of us.

And all the time, Kit says, it was as if Laura knew something awfully important about Jean, which she wouldn't tell him. She was queer and excitable all the afternoon, so that he got worried and actually rather scared. And then she insisted on his going away and leaving her to have a rest."

Fanny nodded. " That's when he came back here. And I told him I didn't know anything at all about Jean's money, except that of course she has rather more of it than most of us, and that she's got a fantastically bad conscience about having it. But I've always taken for granted that that was just because she's such a puritanical, self-torturing sort of person, not because there was anything in the least discreditable about the way she got it. And surely—*surely* Laura wasn't suggesting anything like that."

" I don't know," Susan said. " I haven't any idea what was going on in her mind. Kit hasn't either. But you see, this is what seems to have happened, when Laura sent Kit away. She seems straight away to have made two telephone calls. One was to me. Mummy took it, because I wasn't home yet——"

" We've told them about that," Minnie said. " Fanny and Basil know all about that."

" Well, the second," Susan went on, " seems to have been to Jean. But I'll tell you about that in a minute. About that call to me——" She gave an embarrassed laugh. " I got on my bicycle at once and went to ask Laura what on earth she meant by it. And just outside The Waggoners I saw Jean. She was—well, I don't know how to describe it and I don't want to give you a wrong impression, but there was something awfully odd about the way she was standing there, just as if she didn't want to be seen. And I think she was quite put out at seeing me. And then when I asked her if she was going to see Laura too, she said no, she was looking for Colin. But the fact is, she *was* going to see Laura! "

" How d'you know? " Fanny asked. " Did she say so later? "

" No," Susan said. " She came in with me, and then when I started screaming and behaving like a silly child when I found Laura dead, Jean went very calm and competent, saying she was a nurse and so on, but she still didn't say anything about having to see Laura. All the same, I know she did. You see, I found this—I found it in that cupboard where the telephone is."

She thrust a hand into the pocket of her coat and brought out the envelope addressed to Laura on which the Mordues' and the Gregorys' telephone numbers had been written.

Fanny took it, then handed it to Basil. He looked at it thoughtfully, then handed it on to Tom.

" So you think," Basil said, as Tom turned the envelope this way and that, as if he might succeed in finding more than the two telephone numbers, and keeping Minnie in a fever of impatience to see it, "you think that when Laura had telephoned you, or perhaps even before doing so, she rang up Jean and asked her to come and see her? "

" She may not have asked her to come and see her," Susan said. " After all, she didn't say she wanted to see me. She may just have said something to her that made Jean think she had better go and see her."

" For instance," Basil said, " she may have threatened her with knowledge of some kind and then demanded money."

" Basil! " Minnie cried in a horrified, incredulous tone. " What a terrible thing to suggest! I'm sure Laura Greenslade wasn't that kind of person at all. She was a fine young woman—I know it now, having talked to her. She was a fine, generous-hearted young woman."

" You don't know that you did talk to her," Fanny said.

" Susan," Basil went on gravely, taking no notice of this, " can you tell us anything about how the murder happened? Have the police told you anything? "

" Basil, that's really too much to ask the poor child," Tom said. " Can't you see how upset she is? "

But Susan, upset or not, seemed willing, perhaps even eager, to keep on talking.

" They told me how and when they think it happened," she said. " They think that while Laura was downstairs telephoning, someone slipped up the stairs to her room. You can get to those stairs from the yard where the dust-bins stand, you know, there's no need to go through the bar.

And they think this person hid behind the door of Laura's bedroom and then when she came up, hit her on the head and knocked her unconscious. And then—then stuck a knife in her back. There wasn't any struggle, you see. She didn't cry out. But Basil—Fanny——" She looked from one to the other, the colour in her cheeks mounting slightly. "I didn't tell you all this about Jean to make you think she had anything to do with the murder. It's only that—well, I had to tell someone. I didn't know what to do myself. I found that envelope and I meant to show it to Jean before letting anyone else see it, but when I came out of the telephone cupboard, she'd gone. And I thought the fact that Laura had telephoned Jean was probably important somehow, but still I didn't know whether or not to say anything about it to the police. What ought I to do? Shall I tell them, or shall I just say nothing about it?"

She was looking at Fanny as she finished, but Fanny, with a slight turn of the head, handed the question on to Basil.

A new look of anxiety had appeared on his face while Susan had been speaking. He seemed suddenly to be nervous and restive.

"If I were you, I'd tell the police the whole story," he said. "I don't think it can do any harm."

"I'm quite sure it can't," Minnie said, "since we know who the murderer is. Colin has explained to us——"

"But he was all wrong," Fanny broke in as contemptuously as if she herself had never for a moment accepted Colin's explanation. "Get Basil to tell you—about the phenylthiourea."

Basil had just turned to the door. He looked irritated at being called back, but he paused.

"Oh yes, the phenylthiourea," he said.

"But that had nothing to do with it," Tom said.

"Of course it had something to do with it," Basil replied. "One can accept the idea of just so much coincidence, but more than that. . . . I mean, one can accept the possibility that two people with the idiosyncrasy of being unable to taste it could be in one room at the same time, but that something shockingly bitter-tasting should be prepared for one or other of them and yet phenylthiourea have nothing to do with it, is too much to accept."

" But then, who . . . ? " Minnie said.

" Think of how," Basil said, " and why. Particularly why. And the answer is that that very uncertain method of poisoning Laura Greenslade was used by someone who couldn't afford to meet her face to face. Isn't that the only answer? It was impossible for this person to come into the same room as Laura and slip something into her glass or on to her plate, because that would have meant being recognised by her. But knowing of her peculiarity, it must have seemed at least worth trying to dose the lobster with arsenic and that bitter stuff which would put off everyone else but Laura. Having failed, there was nothing left but simple, violent killing. And now let me remind you, Tom, who it was who managed to pick a quarrel with you, so as to have an excuse at the last moment for not coming to the party."

Incredulously, Fanny exclaimed. " But that was Colin! "

Tom sucked his breath in noisily.

" No, Fanny! " he said. " It was not. I was there and I know who picked the quarrel with me. To do Colin justice, he did all he could to prevent the quarrel."

" But it *couldn't* have been Jean! "

Tom was replying, " But it was, it was," when a loud knock sounded on the front door.

Minnie exclaimed. " Oh, heavens, that must be the police."

Basil went quickly out of the room.

Assuming that he had gone to answer the door, no one else moved, yet after a moment the knock was repeated. Fanny went out into the passage, looked up and down for Basil, and as the knock was repeated once more, called his name softly. There was no reply. Full of disquiet, Fanny went to the door and opened it to let in the police.

CHAPTER NINETEEN

As Basil let himself out by the back door into the garden, he heard Fanny calling him, but he did not answer.

With the door still open, he stood listening till he heard her go to answer the knocking, then he closed the door softly and walked away through the garden. He went towards the gap in the hedge that divided the garden from the Gregorys'. The evening was very dark. The two gardens, lying side by side, looked as if they were all one. Even the trees at the bottom, where the meadows began, scarcely showed against the blackness of the sky.

Basil found the gap by habit and passed through it. In the Gregorys' house the only window with a light behind it was the window of Jean's study. There was no light in the kitchen or in the small sitting-room beside it that was used by the old Polish couple. That meant that they were out for the evening, probably at the cinema. This fact disturbed Basil and made him move faster. He went to the front of the house and without ringing or knocking, tried the door handle. The door was not locked. Opening it quietly, he stepped into the dark hall.

He heard no sound in the house.

After standing there for a moment, listening with a look of troubled indecision on his face, he switched on a light and called out, " Jean—Colin! "

At first there was no answer, then Basil heard slow footsteps overhead and a door open. Colin appeared at the top of the stairs.

He stood there in silence, looking down. Where he stood he was in shadow, for the light, switched on by Basil, illuminated only the hall. Basil could scarcely see his face, but had a feeling that there was some strangeness about it, and something that Colin wished to hide, for he seemed to hold back deliberately where the shadow was deepest.

" Hallo, Basil," he said quietly.

There was a strangeness about his voice too, a curious throaty roughness.

" I came——"

" I know why you came," Colin said. " I've been expecting it sooner or later—you or someone. And now that you're here, you'd better come up. I've something to show you."

There was a deadness in the voice, as well as the roughness.

" All right," Basil said and started to mount the stairs.

Colin turned as Basil reached the top and went ahead of him into Jean's study.

" You see," Colin said, as Basil stopped in the doorway, " you were too late."

At what he saw, Basil felt cold all over, but not really surprised.

" Yes," he said, " too late."

" Or perhaps not. Who knows? " Colin said.

For an instant Basil was able to wrench his eyes away from what was there in the room to Colin's face. He recognised then what had seemed strange about it and understood the unfamiliar quality of the voice. Colin's face was streaked with tears, his eyes were bloodshot and his eyelids swollen.

" Both of them, you see," Colin went on. " She took the baby with her."

Basil could not speak. He stood looking at the terrible thing that seemed to fill every nook and cranny of the small, bare, austere room. His heart felt as if it were beating in slow motion.

Jean was in the chair at the desk. She had fallen forward across it, her shattered head lying on the blotter. The blotter had soaked up some of the blood. One of her arms hung down loosely towards the floor, where, a few inches out of reach of her fingers, lay a revolver. Her other arm lay across the body of her child, which was on her lap. There was no sign of violence on the child. It looked like a little white waxen doll, with staring blue glass eyes.

" How . . . ? " Basil began, but could not go on.

" I think she must have suffocated the child before she shot herself," Colin said in the same lifeless throaty voice. " She left this."

He picked up a sheet of paper from the desk and handed it to Basil.

The paper had a few lines written on it in Jean's clear handwriting.

" This is my own doing. I could not have gone on. Laura rang me up to-day demanding money. I went to see her. There is nothing for me to do now but this. Jean."

Colin was watching Basil intently while he read. When at last Basil looked up, the two men gazed into one another's eyes. A kind of mockery came into Colin's.

" It isn't quite good enough, is it? " he said.

" No, not really," Basil agreed.

" There's an ambiguity in it. She couldn't quite bring herself to accuse herself of murder."

" No."

" Yet she half hoped that that was how it would be taken."

" Yes."

" That's Jean, you know. That's very like Jean. And I'll never know whether she did it like that because she was merely too moral to tell a lie, or whether she was determined, though not quite honest with herself about it, that murder shouldn't go unpunished. It's difficult for me, isn't it, Basil? Can you understand my puzzling about a thing like that at this moment? "

" No," Basil said.

" Ah, that's because you never lived with Jean," Colin said. " I've got into the habit of puzzling over such things. I never knew what she really thought, because she never knew herself, and I was always trying to find the answers she couldn't give me. I always wondered if the real truth was that she hated me."

" Not till the end," Basil said. " At the end I think she did, or she wouldn't have killed the child."

" Yes," Colin said, sounding interested, as if this were a new idea, worth thinking about with care. " I think you must be right. Yes, at the end she hated me. She may have thought—and how could she really think otherwise, being what she was?—that I did it all for the sake of her money."

"Being what she was?" Basil said.

"So unsure of herself," Colin answered, "so uncertain that anyone could really love her."

"But perhaps," Basil said, "she was right."

Colin gave a quick frown. It gave his tear-stained, empty face a querulous fierceness.

"Be careful what you say, Basil."

"I meant," Basil said, "that Jean without her money and the life she could give you with it might not have meant so much to you that you'd have done murder for her sake. Isn't there some truth in that? If you'd loved just Jean herself..."

"Well?"

"No, I may be all wrong about it," Basil said with a sigh. "I confess I don't understand much about murder."

"Which reminds me," Colin said, "I've been meaning to ask you since you came in—when did you decide that I was the murderer?"

"That's a difficult question," Basil said. "I think it was just a few minutes before I came here. But of course I've been thinking about it for some time."

"Then, as soon as you'd decided, you came round here." Colin's lips drew back from his teeth in a stiff, unnatural parody of his usual smile. "That was a rather courageous thing to do, you know."

Basil gave a slight shake of his head. "You've nothing to gain by harming me, have you? I don't believe you actually like harming people. And you've already lost everything that made it seem worth while."

"Yes," Colin said, "that's perfectly true. But then, why did you come?"

"I thought I might be able to help Jean." Basil's eyes dwelt for an instant on the terrible shattered face that rested on the blood-drenched blotter. "I thought I might be able to prevent—something like this."

"I wish you had—I wish to God you had!" Colin cried out. Then his voice dropped again to its quiet, questioning tone. "How did you realise she'd found out the truth?"

"That was from what Susan told me," Basil said. "Susan

saw Jean outside The Waggoners, and she also discovered
that Laura had telephoned Jean. Then she learnt from Kit
that Laura had got extraordinarily excited over seeing Jean,
and had questioned him closely about her money."

" Ah yes, that sounds like Laura." Colin said it as quietly
as before, but with such hatred in his tone that Basil felt he
had never heard this man speak before. It made everything
else that Basil had ever heard his pleasant, good-natured
neighbour say sound shadowy and unreal.

" And out of that you arrived at the fact that I was the
murderer," Colin went on. " That sounds interesting. How
did you do it? "

" Do you mean you really want to know that—now? "

" Yes, naturally."

" Well, as I told you, I'd been thinking about you as the
possible murderer," Basil said, " only I could see no shadow
of reason for your wanting to murder either Laura Greenslade
or Sir Peter Poulter. But it was clear that the poisoning had
been done by someone who had been unable to come to the
party, someone, that's to say, who couldn't afford to come
face to face with whichever of the two it was who had to be
murdered. And that, out of the people who knew enough
about our habits to slip into our kitchen and poison our
food, meant you or Jean, or just possibly Dr. McLean."

" Good God! " Colin exclaimed, sounding genuinely
amazed. " You don't mean you ever suspected him."

" Not very seriously," Basil said. " I learnt that the
accident he'd been called to, the one that prevented his
coming to the party, was perfectly genuine, whereas your
quarrel with Tom had something a little queer and engineered
about it."

" Quarrels with Tom don't take much engineering," Colin
said."

" Perhaps not—but then I realised you'd been behaving
altogether rather queerly recently," Basil said. " You'd been
pursuing a course of action not very characteristic of yourself,
but which was quite certain to lead to trouble with Tom.
And it all began when Fanny told you that Laura was coming
down for the week-end. It was then that you started to take

such a surprising interest in Susan's situation, and decided you must go away to see your friends in Essex about giving her a job. It was while you were away that you got hold of the arsenic and the phenylthiourea, wasn't it? "

Colin nodded. " I must always have underrated you, Basil. It seems you do a lot of observing in your quiet way."

" Well then, you went on behaving in a curious fashion," Basil said. " That quarrel, for instance. I know it was Jean who refused to speak to Tom again and decided that the two of you couldn't come to the party if Tom was coming. But I didn't believe that could have happened if you hadn't wanted it to. You could easily have calmed Jean down if it had suited you to do so. And I remember Jean's telling us how you laughed when she turned on Tom. She was very upset by that laughter. She couldn't understand it. But the truth was, I think, that you couldn't help laughing because your plan was going so beautifully."

" Yes," Colin said, " I'm afraid my self-control slipped up badly there. What other mistakes did I make? "

" I think, on the whole, your continued interference in the course of events," Basil said. " It suggested anxiety. At the same time, everything you did seemed designed to cause trouble. Your attempt to frighten the Mordues, for instance, into behaving suspiciously. It might have succeeded if it hadn't been for Susan. Then you handed on to Fanny what Susan had told you in confidence, and did succeed that time in making trouble between Fanny and Kit. And it was all a little too clever and at the same time too desperate, like your attempt to incriminate poor Clare Forwood."

Colin nodded again.

" Yes," he said. " I was feeling desperate. Yet there was a certain amount of truth in what I said about her and it made a very nice case."

" You knew that she'd been to see Laura? "

" Oh yes, I saw her. I was in the yard when I heard her coming. So I stood back in the shadows till I saw her leave. She was in such a state of shock that she looked quite guilty. She wanted to get away without being seen, without getting involved in any way. It was that that tempted me. You can apologise to her from me, if you like. There was nothing personal in it. I had nothing against her."

" I almost feel," Basil said, " that there's been nothing personal in your attitude to any of us, either love or hate, except to Laura."

" Oh no, I shouldn't like you to think a thing like that about me," Colin said. " I've liked you all very much. But you still haven't told me when you realised the truth about Laura and me."

" I have," Basil said. " I told you, it was just before I came over here. It was when Susan told us all about Laura's telephone call to her and then about how she found an envelope by the telephone in The Waggoners, an envelope that she showed us. It was addressed to Mrs. Charles Greenslade and it had the Mordues' number and yours jotted down on it."

" Laura's call to Susan—what was that about? "

" Laura told Susan that she was handing Kit back to her, breaking off her engagement to him."

" Oh," Colin said. " I see."

" Yes, having seen you in the street this morning with Jean, Laura realised that she couldn't go ahead with her marriage. I suppose that is what happened, isn't it? When she pointed Jean out to Kit in such excitement and wanted to know who she was, you'd actually been with Jean the moment before."

" Yes," Colin said. " We went out together. Then I went into the paper shop to buy cigarettes and Jean went on to do some other shopping. I suppose that's when Laura pointed her out to Kit. It was rash of me to go out at all that day, but I hadn't expected Laura to arrive till the actual day of the inquest. I'd been all prepared to develop 'flu on that day and stay in bed."

" And Laura, on discovering not only that her husband was still alive but bigamously married to a rich woman, realised that this could be a very profitable situation for her —particularly as she could easily prove to Jean that you were responsible for the death of poor old Poulter."

" I was awfully sorry about that, you know," Colin said. "I'd nothing whatever against him. I realised what a crazy thing it had been to try to kill Laura in that way and I decided that next time I'd try something quite simple that couldn't slip up. I pointed that out to you, you know, when I was working out the case against Clare Forwood."

" Yes, you pointed out that the phenylthiourea was really such a crazy thing to have tried that it couldn't possibly be the true explanation."

Another rigid, unnatural little smile tugged at Colin's lips.

" And I thought I was being so ingenious, working that in," he said.

" Too ingenious, too ingenious all the time," Basil said.

" But when did you realise that I was Charles Greenslade? "

" I was very slow about that," Basil said. " It wasn't until I saw the envelope, with your telephone number on it and your initials, C. G.—Colin Gregory or Charles Greenslade. Then things clicked together. Yet I'd known from the first that Laura must have been married already when she was my student. It was her name I remembered her by when Kit produced her and her name hadn't changed. She'd stuck in my mind, of course, because she was an interesting specimen. A homozygous recessive, presumably. Most interesting indeed. But being married, one could be sure that her husband would have been one of the people who'd have heard all about her peculiarity and who'd have remembered it. And it seemed not unlikely too that her husband was a student, and, since it was war-time, and the question of reservation would have arisen, a science student. What was your subject, by the way? "

" I began taking a degree in zoology," Colin said " but I gave it up. I realised I'd never care for that sort of thing. I liked studying the ways of animals and so on, so I thought that meant I was cut out to be a zoologist. A complete mistake, of course. But a worse mistake was meeting Laura in my first week at the university and falling in love with her and marrying her. She was a selfish, scheming, ambitious, empty-headed creature, who decided I'd got to slave my guts out becoming important in some way. After a few weeks I hated her. So I got myself de-reserved and got away into the army. And then—and then I was spending a leave with my mother, whom Laura hated, and a flying-bomb hit the house. I'd gone out only a few minutes before and when I came back there was nothing—nothing left. And in a moment I knew I could vanish. I got into the army again under a false name and got sent to Italy. That was when I met Jean, in hospital. . . ."

His voice faded and he took an uncertain step towards the figure at the desk.

Looking down at it and with his back half-turned to Basil, he said, " It wasn't her money, Basil—I swear it wasn't. It was that she was so awfully good to me. She gave me everything I'd ever wanted."

Suddenly he stooped and picked up the revolver that lay just out of reach of Jean's dead fingers.

" And now you might go, Basil," he said. " You can tell it all to the police and tell them I drove you out at the point of the gun. I'd sooner not do that in fact. I do like you— I like you and Fanny very much. I've nothing whatever against you. So you'll go now, won't you? "

Basil hesitated, then he turned and went out of the room. He went down the stairs and out into the garden. There in the darkness, with a cold wind blowing against him, he stood still.

After a moment he heard the shot.

He gave a convulsive shiver. Then, with his face white from cold and from strain, he started running towards his own home.

THE END